"Howdy!" The g [barcode] wide smile. "You new say we had any new girls comin' on." She walked to the porch rail and extended a hand. "My name's Ruby."

Eliza climbed the steps. Up close, Ruby looked much older than "girl." Considerably so.

"Miss O'Hanlan," the doctor called from the yard below. "Before you go inside, I think—"

"Come on in." Bright smile in place, Ruby held the door open, waiting. "Miss Addie had a fall a little while back so she won't be down here to greet you, but I'll take you up. What'd you say your name was ag'in, hon? Course it don't matter, we'll be changin' it anyway…"

The girl rambled on but Eliza stopped in mid-step. Heavy red drapes with gold trim covered the windows, blocking most of the light and keeping the interior dim. A gold-trimmed mirror all but covered one wall and a life-sized painting of a woman who looked just like Mother wearing a low-cut velvet gown, dominated the first landing.

The cloying aromas of perfume and tobacco mingled to tease her nose along with another muskier scent she couldn't place. "This looks like…" She turned a slow circle, words escaping her.

The doctor bounded up the steps. "Miss O'Hanlan, I think you should know—"

As a prickle of realization moved over her skin, she whirled to face him. "This is a *whorehouse*!"

Praise for Nicole McCaffrey

"Wow! Nicole McCaffrey does it again! Great writing by an amazing author, characters that go straight to your heart [*NORTHERN TEMPTRESS*]."

~The Novel Lady

~*~

"*WILD TEXAS WIND* is an excellent story with a spitfire heroine, a great hero and a wonderful, slightly humorous climax."

~Romantic Times

~*~

"For anyone who appreciates a bad boy cowboy, Raz Colt fits the bill [*WILD TEXAS WIND*]."

~Night Owl Books

~*~

"*SMALL TOWN CHRISTMAS* is syrupy sweet and classically romantic. Holly and Tucker's romantic movie ending is heartwarming and fun."

~Joyfully Reviewed

~*~

"*THE MODEL MAN* is one of the most entertaining books I've read in a long time. I loved every minute of it and will definitely read this one again!"

~Long and Short Reviews

The
Wylder County
Social Club

by

Nicole McCaffrey

The Wylder West

The Wylder County Social Club

Cover Art by *Tina Lynn Stout*

The Wild Rose Press, Inc.
PO Box 708
Adams Basin, NY 14410-0708
Visit us at www.thewildrosepress.com

Publishing History
First Cactus Rose Edition, 2020
Trade Paperback ISBN 978-1-5092-3456-1
Digital ISBN 978-1-5092-3457-8

The Wylder West
Published in the United States of America

Dedication

For Kim,
who nagged—I mean *"encouraged"*—
me to write again

Chapter One

Wylder County, Wyoming
May 1878

Weary of the flat prairie land speeding past the train window, Eliza Jane O'Hanlan glanced at the creased paper in her hand yet again.

The ink was smudged from being clutched in her palm, but the words were still legible. "*Miss Adelaide has been injured in a fall. She has kept up a brave front but needs help running her business in order to give her body time to heal.*"

Nerves fluttered about in her belly like a band of renegade butterflies. She had never been so far from home before, had never dared to dream of coming west. Stories of wild savages and men shooting one another in the street, stories her mother had told her on their few visits over the years, ran rampant through her mind. The thought was more than a little unsettling. She'd been curious about her mother's life and work, intrigued by the urgent request from—she glanced at the letter again—Dr. Samuel Sullivan—though she remained a little uncertain at traveling alone.

Still, her mother needed her. She tried to recall when last she had seen her. Two years? Maybe three? Mother didn't come east often, saying the time away from her business was difficult since she lacked anyone she could trust to run things in her absence.

If she'd sent for her daughter, she must really be in a pickle.

Eliza didn't mind, it was exciting to be needed. For most of her life she'd lived with her spinster aunt, who didn't need care so much as companionship, leaving her to wonder often about the mother who hadn't raised her.

Mother had left her with Aunt Cornelia to head west with her new husband, Farley Willowby, promising to send for her when the time was right, though it seemed that time had never come, not even after Mr. Willowby died, and Mother had been forced to run their business all on her own.

She'd made a success of it, too, from what Eliza learned in her letters. The Wylder County Social Club. It was some sort of home for wayward girls, at least that's what it sounded like from the description. She was proud to think her mother worked so hard on behalf of the downtrodden, even if it did sting to think Mother could put so much love and attention into caring for strangers rather than her own kin. But how clever of her to give it a name that made it sound cheerful and pleasant rather than the orphanage it undoubtedly was.

Eliza knew nothing of caring for children, let alone wayward ones, but for Mother's sake, she would roll up her sleeves and help out wherever needed.

The train whistle sounded and as the car chugged to a halt in the Wylder depot, she pulled in a deep breath. There would undoubtedly be awkward feelings at first; after all, she and her mother were nothing more than friendly strangers who exchanged letters. They would need time to get to know one another.

She stepped off the train into the depot. A few other passengers were disembarking and she scanned the faces for anyone who appeared to be waiting for someone. Her passage had been arranged by this Doctor Sullivan, but there was no elderly gentleman in the crowd.

"Need help with yer bags, ma'am?"

She turned to see a tall, fair-haired young man about her own age. Though Aunt Cornelia had warned her to be wary of strangers while traveling alone, this one was dressed in clean, pressed trousers and shirt, and seemed harmless enough.

"Why yes, thank you." Her voice wavered a bit and she hoped her nervousness didn't show.

He grinned and picked up her luggage. "You don't look familiar a'tall. You new in town?"

"Yes. I've come here to help my—" Mother was a proud woman, maybe she wouldn't want the townspeople to know she needed help. "I've come here to work."

Her companion fell into step beside her. "Lots of prospects here in Wylder, ma'am."

"Oh, I'm not looking for work, in fact I already have a destination in mind. I was hoping someone would be meeting me here, but I don't see anyone." She paused to scan the small sea of people. There were cowboys, men in dark blue soldier's uniforms, women going about their business, clutching the hands of small children, and people greeting loved ones with great enthusiasm. But none seemed to be looking for someone else. She turned back to her companion. "Perhaps you could offer me directions?"

"Sure thing, ma'am. Or I could just take you there

m'self. Where ya headed?" They continued on, making their way through the crowd.

She jumped back as a rider on a horse rushed past, narrowly missing her but leaving her dark brown traveling skirt and boots splattered with mud. "The Wylder County Social Club."

A hush fell over the people nearby. Two women stopped mid-conversation and turned to glare at her. A man passing by was so intent on staring he walked splat into another man who was doing the same.

What funny people they were here in Wylder. And perhaps a bit nosey. Did all strangers to visit the town capture their attention so completely?

Her companion stopped, dropped her bags and grinned. He removed his hat, and boldly looked her over from head to toe. "Why yes, ma'am. I'll be sure to come and pay a visit."

"I'm sure I'd appreciate that, Mister—"

"Ezra Barlow," a deep voice said from behind them. "And he was just leaving."

Eliza turned to see a tall man with broad shoulders and dark hair that fell past the collar of his coat.

"Now Doc, you gonna have to wait your turn with the rest." The young Mister Barlow wagged a finger at him. "I seen her first."

The dark-haired man's hand went to his hip, pulling back his coat enough to reveal the revolver holstered there. "You ever shoot a man, Barlow?"

The younger man took a slight step back. "N—no sir."

"Well I have. Dozens of 'em during the war. Won't bother me a bit to shoot another." The deep voice rumbled with authority. "Go on, now. Skedaddle."

Ezra scurried off, leaving Eliza to consider the man before her. She'd noticed his height and rather long hair before, but now she saw the few days' growth of stubble on his face was sprinkled with a bit of gray. She guessed him to be in his mid-thirties. Surely this wasn't the Doctor Sullivan who had written to her; she was expecting a much older man. "Did I understand Mr. Barlow to call you 'Doc'?"

He touched the brim of his black hat, green eyes scanning the length of her. "Yes, ma'am. I'm sorry I'm late, I was helping birth a colt at the Holt ranch."

"I see."

Doc picked up the bags Barlow had abandoned, and she fell into step alongside him until they came to an elaborate wagon with a padded leather seat. "This is lovely."

"I spend a lot of time riding around town and the surrounding areas," he said. "It helps to have a comfortable seat."

"Yes." She eyed the step up into the wagon, wondering how to do so gracefully in the long, straight traveling skirt. "About that. I was under the impression you were a medical doctor."

He reached to set her bags in the back. "I am. But I help anywhere I'm needed."

Eliza couldn't take her eyes from the gun that peeked out from under the coat when he moved. "And that?"

A slow grin crossed his face. "I keep forgetting you've lived back east your whole life."

"Then I guess you have the advantage; I know nothing about you other than you are the one who sent for me." She studied the step again. There wasn't much of a choice but to hike her skirt and get it over with. She glanced around to see how many would witness the spectacle.

He placed his hands to his hips, studying her. "Want some help?"

A flush came over her, embarrassed that he had noted her predicament. "No."

"Most women here don't wear such fussy clothing." He gestured toward her outfit. "It's not practical here on the frontier."

"Well, I am not from here, now am I?" And with that she placed one foot onto the step, hoisted her skirt, and plopped into the seat. She didn't dare look to see who had noticed.

He climbed up alongside her and took up the reins, clicking his tongue for the horse to move forward. "Let's go, Harley." She knew nothing of horses, but this one had a shiny red coat, black mane and white nose and seemed quite tame. They pulled out of the depot onto a well-worn dirt road, the rhythmic clip clop of horse hooves blending with the activity around them.

The bustling town was very different from New York. She missed the greenery of the trees, the oasis of shade cast by the giant maples and elms. Here everything looked so new and unfinished. She pulled her gaze away from the trees as church bells sounded in the distance, reminding her it was Sunday. "How is my mother?"

"She's fine, stubborn as he—ever. Still trying to run the whole place from her bed." He cleared his throat. "I mean, even though she's bedridden."

"I see. And the business itself has not suffered from her absence?" Were the girls in Mother's care suffering from neglect in her convalescence? How that must upset her.

"Not a mite, it's as busy as ever." He glanced at her and then ahead to the busy road once more.

"My goodness. There must be a lot of wayward girls in need of care. Is there nowhere else in town they could stay temporarily?"

He looked over at her and frowned. "Just how much do you know about your mother's business?"

"Well, as you stated before, I've lived back east my entire life. Mother and I write from time to time and she visits when she can." She glanced down at the hands in her lap, careful to keep any bitterness from her voice. *Letters and visits were a poor substitute for a mother.* "Of course those are social affairs, she doesn't talk much about business other than to say things are going well."

"I see." He cleared his voice and fidgeted with the reins, his jaw tightening. Had she said the wrong thing? "Mother does know I'm coming, doesn't she?"

"Nope." His reply came as an abrupt retort.

She waited but he didn't seem inclined to offer more than that. He stared straight ahead. "Wh—why didn't you tell her?"

He chuckled and shook his head. "If Miss Addie knew someone was coming to take over running her place, she'd be out of that bed, broken ankle or not. Just to spite anyone who dared to suggest she couldn't do it."

"I see." Though she really didn't. Was he saying Mother didn't want help?

"She's a stubborn woman, Miss O'Hanlan. But she's getting on and it's not a sign of weakness to ask for help. Thing is, if she doesn't stay off that ankle, she's never going to walk properly again."

Nervous flutters began in her stomach again. She didn't know her mother well enough to put her foot down with her, but it was apparent she'd need to try. "Are we nearly there?"

"Almost." He nodded ahead.

"But we're leaving the center of town." She turned to glance behind her, disappointed at not seeing the rest of Wylder, though she supposed there would be time for that.

He clicked his tongue urging the horse further. "It's just across the tracks. Last place you come to."

She frowned. An odd location for a thriving business. But given the success, Mother must have known what she was doing by placing it there.

The buggy jostled as it crossed the railroad tracks. She stared as a two-story clapboard house with a wide inviting porch came into view.

"Why, this is lovely." A young woman sat in a rocker on the veranda. Was this one of the wayward girls mother cared for? As they drew closer, she noticed the girl's dress was a bit fancy for this time of day, cut low enough to reveal much of her bosom. And the heavily rouged cheeks—on a Sunday, no less. Oh, Mother must really have her hands full with this one.

The wagon drew to a stop. The doctor turned in his seat to look at her. "Miss O'Hanlan. I think there's something—"

The girl on the porch rose and waved enthusiastically. "Afternoon, Doc."

He acknowledged the woman with a touch to the brim of his hat.

She giggled and swayed from side to side, almost childlike in her enthusiasm. "You here on business—or pleasure?"

Eliza climbed down from the buggy as gracefully as she could and stood in the yard, staring up at the house while the doctor collected her bags.

"Howdy!" the girl said, regarding Eliza with a wide smile. "You new here, honey? Miss Addie didn't say we had any new girls comin' on." She walked to the porch rail and extended a hand. "My name's Ruby."

Eliza climbed the steps. Up close, Ruby looked much older than "girl." Considerably so.

"Miss O'Hanlan," the doctor called from the yard below. "Before you go inside, I think—"

"Come on in." Bright smile in place, Ruby held the door open, waiting. "Miss Addie had a fall a little while back so she won't be down here to greet you, but I'll take you up. What'd you say your name was ag'in, hon? Course it don't matter, we'll be changin' it anyway..."

The girl rambled on but Eliza stopped in mid-step. Heavy red drapes with gold trim covered the windows, blocking most of the light and keeping the interior dim. A gold-trimmed mirror all but covered one wall and a life-sized painting of a woman who looked just like Mother wearing a low-cut velvet gown, dominated the first landing.

The cloying aromas of perfume and tobacco mingled to tease her nose along with another muskier scent she couldn't place. "This looks like..." She turned a slow circle, words escaping her.

The doctor bounded up the steps. "Miss O'Hanlan, I think you should know—"

As a prickle of realization moved over her skin, she whirled to face him. "This is a *whorehouse*!"

Chapter Two

The girl before him swayed, and Coyote caught her a split second before she hit the ground. Why hadn't he seen this coming? He scooped her into his arms, carrying her into the parlor while Ruby ran to fetch his bag from the buggy.

By now the rest of Miss Adelaide's girls had gathered, whispering among themselves and expressing concern. He laid the young woman out on the settee, propping her feet up on the rolled arm. Ruby returned, holding the bag out to him, hovering nearby by as he dug out his smelling salts and stethoscope.

By now Miss O'Hanlan had begun to mumble incoherently. He waved the salts under her nose, relieved when she recoiled and pushed his hand away. He should have guessed the shock would be too much for her.

"Easy now," he cautioned when she tried to sit up. "Could one of you ladies fetch a glass of cool water and a wet cloth?"

Miss Addie's daughter continued to look around, her eyes wide with fear and shock. He took a good look at her pupils, relieved to see they were normal size. "Do you know where you are?"

Her frightened gaze flew back to his face. "I... thought I did. Why did you bring me h—here?"

"I think maybe we'd best let Miss Addie explain

that." He raised his stethoscope for her to see. "Mind if I take a listen?"

For the first time he noticed the soft cornflower blue of her eyes. She was no spring chicken; he'd bet she was in her late twenties, possibly older. But the reddish-gold hair pulled into a severe knot at the back of her neck showed no gray, and her pale skin was unblemished. After a moment of hesitation, she nodded.

He settled the diaphragm on her chest and listened. Her heartbeat was bounding, about what he'd expect for the shock and fear she must be feeling, but otherwise normal.

She stared wide-eyed over his shoulder where whispers and speculation from the girls who had gathered carried to them. When he finished, he glanced behind him to see that the ladies had begun to inch closer. As curious about Miss O'Hanlan as she was about them, no doubt.

Ruby came back into the room, cup and cloth in hand.

"You can sit up to drink," he told the young woman, "but don't try to stand just yet." He waited for her to nod.

He sensed rather than saw the girls behind them move closer. He turned to look over his shoulder. "Why don't you ladies give her some room to catch her breath, she's had quite a shock."

When they only stared, Ruby clapped her hands. "Ya heard the doc. Go on now. Git. All of ya."

They reluctantly began to move away, but the muffled chatter continued.

"Didn' she know where she was comin' to work?" whispered someone behind him.

"I don't think she's workin' here," said another.

"Who is she?"

"Darned if I know..."

At last they had gone and he studied Miss O'Hanlan while she sipped the water and looked about the room. The ornate furnishings and deep red wallpaper probably looked very out of place to her. "This really is a... house of ill repute?"

"There's lots of names for it, ma'am," he said, placing his things back into his bag. "Hog ranch. Cat house. Den of sin. You didn't know?"

She shook her head and rested the cup on the hand in her lap. "No."

He winced. "Sorry. If I'd known that I never would have sent for you. I just assumed her family knew."

He continued to arrange the things in his bag, mostly for something to do while he weighed his next words. "I guess you'll be going back home then. The train only comes in on Sundays, so you'll have to wait a week. You could check Miss Culpepper's boarding house for a room. Or the Wylder Hotel."

She stared at the floor beside him, as if searching for something. Gradually, her furrowed brow softened and her chin came up. The blue gaze that met his was determined, if nothing else. "I'd like to see my mother now."

****

Eliza trailed a hand along the dark wood rail on the way up the stairs. The smell of lemon oil was overpowering. Her feet sank into the rich dark red carpeting on the stairs and landing. At the top of the first staircase, she paused. There was the portrait she'd noticed before, the one of a woman who looked like her

13

mother, but not in a way that she'd ever seen her. Her hair was an unnatural shade somewhere between white and pale yellow, the gown she wore dipped low between her breasts and her face was heavily painted. But naggingly familiar even after all this time.

"Are you all right?"

She'd sensed the doctor behind her every step of the way; she suspected he was worried she would pass out again. And maybe she would. She'd never fainted before, but the days of travel had taken their toll. And now... this.

"Fine. I just don't know her like... *that*." She gazed up at the second staircase and pulled in a steadying breath before placing her foot on the next step. "Her hair was brown whenever I saw her. No face paint." So the mother she'd only known from afar wasn't even real.

The touch of his hand on her elbow was a welcome comfort. "This is how all of Wylder knows her, Miss O'Hanlan."

As a whore.

The idea stole into her mind before she could stop it. Had Aunt Cornelia known? There had always been a tone of disapproval whenever she spoke of Mother, but Eliza had assumed it was due to her mother all but abandoning her.

"You don't have to do this now."

She glanced back at the doctor. His green eyes were soft as he regarded her, still holding that lingering concern. He was handsome, she'd noted that in the train depot. But the comfortable way that firearm rested on his hip, the dark hair that reached to his shoulders, the carefree growth of stubble, all hinted at a man far too rough to be tamed.

Not that she would ever try to tame one. She wouldn't know where to begin.

Any doctor she'd ever met had been far older, far less... masculine.

This man seemed as wild and primitive as the land on which he lived. A warm flush moved over her. Now where had that silly notion come from? Perhaps he was just too busy to see a barber.

His hand came to rest on her elbow again, the heat from it penetrating her sleeve. "Why don't you sit for a minute and catch your breath."

"I'm fine." She shook her head. "If I don't do this now, I may not ever have the courage."

She made her way up the rest of the stairs, her stomach twisting in knots.

"That you, Ruby?"

Funny how even after years of not seeing her mother, she still knew her voice. "No ma'am. I—It's me." She closed her eyes and swallowed hard. "Eliza Jane."

A beat of silence followed, then a yelp of dismay.

A nudge from behind sent her stumbling toward the open door.

Inside the room, a small woman sat in a giant four poster mahogany bed. The canopy and bed coverings were all various shades of pink, as was the elaborate dressing gown, as fancy as anything Eliza had ever seen.

Mother's eyes grew wide. "Land sakes, child, what are you do—you might'a told a body you were comin'!"

"I sent for her, Miss Adelaide." The doctor stepped

into the doorway, leaned against the doorframe, bag and hat in hand. "I warned you if you didn't take it easy, I'd send for help."

"I did take it easy," she protested. "Least as much as I could see to. But dang it all, Coyote, I never gave you permission to contact my daughter. I didn't even know you knew where to find her."

"All things you can yell at me for another day, Addie," he said. "But first I'm going to leave you two alone to talk. Miss Eliza, I'll be right downstairs when you're ready to leave." His gaze met hers, warm and reassuring. "I'll take you anywhere you want to go."

Somehow Eliza found her voice. "Thank you."

Doctor Sullivan glanced back to Mother. "She's had quite a shock, keep that in mind."

Eliza watched his retreating back, unable to keep from admiring his broad shoulders as he departed. She wanted to call him back, ask him to stay. For reasons she couldn't comprehend, his presence soothed her.

But her family problems were not his concern. She sat on the foot of the bed, unable to help taking in her surroundings. When she could avoid it no longer, she glanced at her mother's face, studying the paint and rouge, the platinum hair. This was not the woman who had visited her so few times in the past. "Why didn't you tell me?"

Miss Adelaide's shrug was almost childlike. "And give that busybody sister of mine the satisfaction of knowing she was right about Farley?"

Eliza shook her head, unable to stop the thoughts racing through her mind, or slow them long enough to catch one. "I don't even know what to ask, where to begin."

She rose to her feet, rubbing her arms to ward off a sudden chill. Her thoughts continued to flit about like fireflies, until finally from deep in the pit of her stomach a familiar pain began. She pressed a hand to her mouth to stifle a sob. "All those years waiting for you to come for me. It was bad enough thinking you were caring for orphaned girls—that you chose them over me. But...this?" She gestured wildly about the room. "I don't understand, Mama."

"Eliza, sit, let me talk to you." Adelaide reached out her arms. "Slow down and give me time to explain."

The open door beckoned to her; she rushed toward it. "I can't. I can't do this right now."

She hurried toward the stairs, but sunlight streaming through a window at the end of the long hallway caught her attention. Curious, cautious, half-afraid one of the bedroom doors would open and some roughhewn cowboy would accost her, she continued heading toward the refuge of another staircase, this one much less elaborate. She hurried down it, keeping her footsteps light.

She had just reached the bottom when someone wielding an iron skillet like a weapon sprang out.

Chapter Three

Eliza raised her hands to protect herself at the same moment the other woman screamed.

When no blow came, she cautiously peeked through raised arms. A familiar face came into sight, though older than the last time they had met. Her heart leapt in her chest. "Mrs. McCarthy?"

The older woman put a hand to her chest and lowered her pan. "Eliza Jane O'Hanlan," she said in a thick Irish brogue. "Good Lord, child, I nearly killed ya!"

She glanced over her shoulder to see if anyone was behind her. "Did you think I was someone else?"

"Yes and no." She put an arm about Eliza's shoulders and guided her into the room. Eliza noted a tidy room in shades of white and gray, with copper pots and pans on the stove and a wooden table with six chairs around it.

The kitchen door burst open and Doctor Sullivan stood there, gun poised and ready.

Mrs. McCarthy waved a dismissive hand. "I'm all right, Sam. No cowboys sneaking out the back way this time."

His gaze swept the room before landing back on the two of them. "I heard screaming."

"Me," Eliza confessed. "I startled Mrs.—"

"Aoife," the older woman corrected.

"Aunty Ee-fee." Whenever Mother had visited, the warm, friendly Irish woman had accompanied her. But Eliza had been unable to pronounce her name. A lump of emotion lodged in her throat at the memory of the hugs and kisses Aoife had lavished on her during those visits.

The older woman's blue eyes sparkled. "Now, child, you're old enough to say it right. Eee-fah."

"Aunt Aoife." At one time, Eliza had believed her to be her mother's personal maid. Now, it seemed that was yet another lie. "You're not surprised to see me."

If possible, the rosy cheeks reddened.

Doctor Sullivan holstered his weapon with confident ease. "Eef's the one who told me how to reach you." He stepped into the room. "I think you can guess why your mother didn't want that."

A thump and cry sounded from overhead.

"Oh Lord, what now?" Aoife threw her hands up. "The house isn't even open for the day yet."

Sullivan tensed. "Adelaide." He rushed toward the stairs.

Eliza followed, Aunt Aoife at her heels, all heading back up the stairs once more.

They found Adelaide on the floor in her room, howling in pain. A cane was just out of her reach.

Sullivan scooped her up into his arms like she weighed nothing more than a sack of flour and laid her on the bed. "What did you do? Addie, I've told you a dozen times—"

"My girls." She winced, trying to reach her lower leg, which was splinted and tied. "I heard one of 'em scream."

"That was me, you foolish girl," Aoife said,

stepping forward and pulling the blankets up. "You don't start listenin' to the doc, we'll never get you outta that bed."

"Eef, bein' in this bed has made me a very wealthy—"

"Hush now in front of the girl!"

Realizing Aunt Aoife was talking about her, Eliza stepped fully into the room.

"My baby girl," Adelaide's reached for her. I can't believe you're really here. I didn't get a good look at you before. C'mere, let Mama see you."

The doctor shook his head. "You can get a good long look at her later, Addie. Right now I need to examine that ankle and make sure you didn't do more damage."

A glint came into Adelaide's eyes. "Doc, if I was about twenty years younger, I'd examine you right back."

Aoife huffed and waved a hand in the air. "Enough of that nonsense. Eliza, dear, let's go put the kettle on. What do you take in your tea?"

Eliza allowed herself to be steered into the hall, glancing back at her mother, uncertain if she should leave. "Um… cream and sugar."

"Brandy it is, then."

Chapter Four

Satisfied that Adelaide hadn't managed to do any further damage, Coyote headed down the back stairway once again.

Aoife and Eliza sat at the small wooden table chatting over cups of tea. When she looked up, Eliza's smile was overly warm and her eyes a bit glassy.

"How's our girl?" Aoife asked.

The Irishwoman's face was rosy and he guessed there was more than tea in those cups. "Resting," he said. "I gave her some laudanum; she'll be out for a while."

"Cuppa tea?" she asked, holding up the pot.

"I prefer my brandy straight," he answered with a chuckle. He glanced over at Eliza, who drained the contents of her cup, then held it out for more.

"You sure that's wise?" he asked, meeting Aoife's gaze.

"She's had such a shock, poor girl," the older woman *tsked* as she refilled the cup.

He placed his hands to his hips. "You're the one who told me how to reach her."

"That's why you didn't ask why I was here." Eliza hiccupped, then put her hands to her lips and giggled. "When you saw me at the bottom of the stairs. You wer—" she hiccupped again. "Weren't surprised to see me. Not one bit."

Aoife shot him a startled look. "Don't be tellin' your mother that," she said.

He frowned, studying the girl at the table. "Miss Eliza, are you feeling all right?"

"I feel wunnerful," she insisted, draining the cup yet again. "This is the best tea I've ever had."

"If you'll recall, ma'am, you wanted to leave and find another place to stay until the train comes again next week," he reminded her, but it appeared the alcohol had affected her sense of things.

"Oh yes, yes." She started to rise, swayed and plopped back down. "I don't feel so very well."

"Perhaps you should lie down, dear," Aoife suggested. "My room is just over there, off the kitchen."

He helped the older woman get the girl to her room, even as she protested over all the fuss.

"I'll just lie here for a few moments." But even as she said the words, her eyes were drifting closed. "I'm glad you are here, Auntie Eefee... makes it...easier. To learn about Mother, I mean."

Aoife patted her hand. "I'll bring you something to eat in a little while, my dear, you just rest."

When they stepped out of the room, Aoife cast him a frustrated glance. "I know it was wrong to send for the girl when she didn't know the truth, but Adelaide needs her. Maybe they both need each other."

Coyote lit a cigarillo and pulled the smoke deep into his lungs. "There are more than a few girls here who are capable of helping her. You know it and so do I."

Aoife waved a dismissive hand. "No matter how much they feel like family, those girls are still just employees. Adelaide needs help from her own kin. And it's high time that girl got to know her mother. It will do them both some good."

"You're messin' where you shouldn't be messin, Eef—you're up to something."

Aoife chuckled. "Oh, go on with you. And take that nasty smoke out of here."

****

The rattle and clatter of pots and pans woke Eliza. She sat up, glancing around in bewilderment. A small bed with a chair just beside it were the lone occupants of the room. A yellow curtain embroidered with daisies covered the window but sunlight streamed through the cheery little room.

Pain rushed through her head as she swung her feet to the floor.

Aoife poked her head inside the door. "Good mornin' to you," she greeted. "Can I get you some coffee?"

Eliza nodded, trying to piece together how she had come to be here. She reached up to her hair, dismayed to find it disheveled. "Did I sleep all night?"

Aoife set the coffee on the table in the kitchen with a thunk. "That ya' did. Now then, the girls will be down here for breakfast before long. The place opens for business at ten today."

"In the morning?" She began to pull the pins from her hair, patting as she went, frowning that some of them seemed to have twisted into knots, until she found them all.

"Yes, hard as it is to believe," Aoife said as she bustled about the kitchen. "But the soldiers from the fort keep us busy on their days off. By evening, the men from town and the surrounding ranches filter in."

A sizzling sound came and with it the smells of bacon frying. Her stomach began to roil. She still hadn't fully decided what she was going to do about her situation, but either way it looked as though she was stuck here for a week. Still, she couldn't very well run a brothel.

She rose and headed toward the kitchen. "How do the er, ladies, manage to… accommodate all of them?"

The woman waved a dismissive hand. "Oh, they have their ways I suppose."

Eliza frowned at the evasive tone. "I'll just step outside and use the necessary." She headed for the back door. Just as she put her hand on the knob, there was a knock and then it opened.

She stepped back at the sight of the handsome doctor.

"Mornin' Sam," called Aoife, as if she'd been expecting him.

"Mornin, Eef.…" He glanced at her and his eyes widened in surprise. "Miss Eliza."

Heat rushed her cheeks. She must look a fright with her hair hanging wild about her shoulders. She reached up to smooth it into place as best she could. "I'm afraid I'm just getting up and about. If you'll excuse me."

She returned a short time later, a bit dismayed to find the doctor still there. Ruby, the girl she met yesterday, had come down to the kitchen, as well as several of the other girls. A flash of something almost like jealousy stabbed at her as she saw the way Ruby gazed intently at the doctor, seeming to hang on his every word.

He held a small vial in his hand. Both looked up as she came into the room.

"Miss Adelaide usually mixes the drinks, so maybe you could tell Miss Eliza?" Ruby gave her a big smile. "You look real pretty with your hair down like that."

"Will you be makin' the drinks?" asked a caramel-skinned girl with jewel green eyes. Emerald? Was that her name?

Why were the drinks so important in a house of ill repute? "I...I don't know."

"It's just we don't wanna get the dosage wrong and you know, knock them out for too long," the girl said. "Or worse."

"I don't under..."

"The medicine," Ruby continued. "Miss Addie knows just how many drops for what size man will knock him out and for how long. None of us have ever had to do it. I don't wanna kill no one."

"Medicine?" Eliza looked from the doctor to Aoife. Both looked away.

"Yes," Ruby took the vial from the doctor's hand and held it up for her to see. "Doc brings it by every week."

Sullivan rose from his chair at the table. "Maybe I should explain exactly what it's for." He gestured toward the door.

Eliza followed, a knot forming in her stomach that grew by the second.

They stepped into the outdoors, the blinding sun reminding her once more that she didn't feel quite right this morning. She had barely taken her foot off the bottom step when he turned to face her. "It's not what you think." His deep voice rumbled through her.

She folded her arms. "Then tell me what I should think, *doctor*."

He exhaled a loud sigh. "Some of the soldiers can get a bit… rough. They start swapping war stories and things can get outta hand fast. Your mama needed something that would help calm them down, make them feel a little sleepy. That's all."

She didn't understand any of this. "And you provide this…medicine?"

He held her gaze. "Yes."

"So judging from the vial Ruby showed me, the women expect a great many of these rough soldiers?" She shuddered at the idea.

He stroked a hand down his beard, as though he'd rather be anywhere but here. "No, now hear me out."

She couldn't help the impatient foot that began to pat the ground. "I am listening, Doctor Sullivan."

He gave her the hint of a smile. "Friends call me Coyote."

"I don't intend to be here long enough to make friends, thank you." She paced away a few steps. "You were explaining why my mother needs so much of this…medicine?"

With a heavy sigh, he glanced up at the sky. "Because they knock out most all the men now."

She stared at him for long moments before she could find her voice. "Y—you're saying that these men come her for…for…but instead…?"

"The less I know the better, but that's the way I understand it." He studied her with eyes the color of new grass. "Yes."

"And you, a doctor, are complicit in this?" She shook her head. "It's bad enough I get called upon to help run a whorehouse without my knowledge. But now I'm expected to take part in drugging and deception, too?"

She whirled toward the house but stopped halfway up the steps. "You should all be ashamed of yourselves. But none more so than you, *Doctor* Sullivan."

Chapter Five

Coyote slid into a stool at the bar and glanced up at the bartender. "Make it a double, Cash."

The man nodded.

"Little early in the day for a drink?" asked a nearby patron.

Coyote turned to see Russ Holt. "It is." Cash set the drink before him, and he raised the glass to his lone saloon companion before tossing back the contents.

"Let me guess," Holt said, a lazy smile turning up the corners of his gray moustache. "A woman?"

Coyote groaned. "Several of them. And one in particular."

He was still trying to get the image of Eliza out of his head. She'd changed out of the stuffy traveling outfit she'd had on yesterday into a simple cotton dress. But it was the long, reddish gold hair that hung in waves to her waist that had caught his attention this morning. She was a beauty, though he should have expected no less, given her mother's good looks.

I don't intend to be here long enough to make friends.

Why did those words bother him so much? He had no interest in befriending her. Hell, no interest of any kind in her, he'd done his part and sent for her. The rest was up to her and Adelaide.

But the way she'd judged him for supplying

Adelaide with the necessary means to keep the clientele under control still nagged at him.

She didn't know the situation at all, how raucous drunk soldiers and cowboys could get. Had likely never seen someone die from syphilis or from a self-induced abortion. Brothels served a purpose, but the unknown side of such places could be ugly. Abuse, broken bones, death.

He'd seen enough suffering and dying in the war, treated enough of the diseased whores who followed the army camps to know about their illnesses and how young they died.

Miss Adelaide's unique way of doing business might not be exactly moral, but it kept everyone healthy and alive.

With any luck, Eliza would realize that by the end of the night.

The thought left a coil of unease in his stomach. The town was already buzzing with news of her arrival. Most assumed she was working at Miss Addie's place, so there would be a crowd tonight, all clamoring for a look at the new girl.

His fault, the knot in his gut reminded him. He'd sent for her. Well, Aoife had insisted after Adelaide had all but exhausted herself trying to run things from the bed and not getting the rest she needed.

In the end, the truth was Ruby and the other girls simply weren't business women. They knew nothing of what it took to run a business and things were getting out of hand in a hurry. Which was likely why Aoife had nearly clocked Eliza over the head with that frying pan yesterday; too many clients making a run for it down the back stairs.

The Wylder Social Club needed its Madam back—and soon.

But the image of Eliza's hair hanging loose to her waist nagged at him. As buttoned-up and uptight as she initially appeared, he'd never have guessed she'd be that beautiful with her hair down. For a moment there, she'd all but taken his breath.

He still couldn't shake the feeling that he was responsible for her. Maybe he should stop by tonight, mainly to check on Miss Addie's ankle, but to ease his mind about how well Eliza was able to handle herself. Or at least offer to pay for her return ticket to New York.

He strode over to the table where Russ sat.

Holt raised his glass in greeting. "Drinking this early in the day, it's always about a woman."

"I could say the same to you," Coyote pointed out. "Miss Adelaide still keeping you at arm's length?" The fact that Miss Addie and Russ Holt, one of the town's most successful ranchers, were intimately involved was one of the town's biggest open secrets. But since her injury, Addie wouldn't allow him to visit.

Before Russ could answer, the doors were pushed open again and a young man burst in, looking frantically about. "The doc in here?"

Coyote jumped to his feet.

"Ya gotta come quick, Doc," the man shouted. "The mill. Red McCleary done cut off half his hand."

****

Eliza faced her mother, waiting for an answer. Didn't she deserve at least that much?

"It ain't like that." Adelaide frowned at her. "Not what you're thinkin' anyway."

"What I think is taking money from gentleman for…services…they don't actually receive is stealing." She folded her arms. "Do you even know what's in this medicine? What exactly are you giving these men?"

"It's all natural," Adelaide insisted. "Nothin' that'll harm them. Coyote gets it from some Indian lady. It's herbs and such."

"And that's another thing. Involving the doctor in your scheme. What were you thinking?" She shook her head. "Doctors are sworn by oaths to do no harm, for goodness sake."

"Now don't go gettin' all sanctimonious and judgey like your Aunt Cornelia."

"If I'm acting like her, it's because you left her to raise me."

Adelaide flinched. "I suppose I had that comin'."

"Oh Mother, I didn't mean it." Eliza sighed, regretting the hastily uttered words.

"Yes, you did, and I deserve it." Addie made a show of smoothing the blanket, but Eliza could see her eyes had gone watery.

"I shouldn't have said it, though. This isn't the time to pick at old wounds." She strode to the bed and took a seat at the foot, running a hand up the fine mahogany bedpost, marveling at the craftsmanship. It must have cost a fortune.

"You don't understand our ways, is all," Addie said, her face softening.

She sighed and rested a cheek against the smooth wood. "The doctor said some of the men get rough."

"Rough ain't the word. Some of 'em get so overexcited they can't control themselves. Or they start fightin' each other. If I have to hear that damn war

31

fought one more time…" She shook her head. "The medicine was never supposed to be a regular thing."

Eliza slid a glance over at her. "But?"

"But well…" Adelaide looked thoughtful. "It was just easier. First, we started just knocking out the rowdy ones. Then, from a business standpoint, it just made sense to keep on doin' it."

Maybe if she could make sense of it, she could understand it. "How do you mean?"

"The girls can see twice as many men in a night. We ain't changin' the sheets a dozen times a day, which saves on washin'. And the girls stay healthy." Her chin came up. "Do you know my place is noted in *The Gentlemen's Blue Book* as bein' one of the cleanest clubs in all of Wyoming? No diseases here."

Eliza gave a small laugh. "I would imagine not."

"It ain't just the money though. I…I lost someone dear to me once. One of my girls." Addie looked away, as though the memory was too painful to face.

"From illness?" Eliza asked.

"No, it was—" the resonant bonging of the grandfather clock in the hallway downstairs interrupted. "Lord, girl, we open in an hour," she said after the chiming had stopped. "You'll need a gown and some instruction on what to do."

Eliza shot to her feet, shocked at the very suggestion. "You don't honestly think I'm going to entertain men?"

"Not in the way my girls do, but yes, someone has to keep them busy while they wait their turn. And if they come in not knowing which girl they want to see, you have to help them figure it out." Addie looked thoughtful. "Sometimes I play piano or sing—can you sing?"

"Mother, I am not trussing myself up like a strumpet and entertaining men." Eliza's voice climbed an octave at the horror of that particular picture. "Not today, not ever."

Adelaide gave her a critical glance. "I suppose you ain't got the build for it. You're far too uppity anyway. Well, Opal and Pearl are both good at entertainin'. They can take turns with that part of it. But you'll have to mix the drinks."

****

The tinkling of a piano, played by a traveling musician who passed through the area every few months, accompanied the singing and antics of Opal and Ruby. The two made a great show of entertaining the male guests who awaited the girl of their choice by dancing, singing ribald songs, and wisecracking in-between.

From a safe distance across the room, Eliza kept a steady eye on the door as more and more men spilled in.

"Just greet them and ask if they're here to see anyone special," Aoife whispered. "And whatever you do, don't turn your back on 'em and don't let 'em pin you in a corner."

Abraham, the bouncer, stood silently watchful. A large, heavily muscled, dark-skinned man, he stood well over six feet tall. His face remained expressionless as his dark eyes darted from guest to guest, though more than once he caught Eliza's gaze and gave her a reassuring nod. His presence was indeed comforting.

The bell over the door jangled. Eliza drew a breath and ran her hands over her skirt. Unlike the other girls, the neckline of her dress came up to her chin. But that didn't stop the soldiers who stomped through the door from eyeing her like a sweet confection.

A soldier approached her, his wide grin and knowing gaze making her stomach turn. "Well, hello there, darlin', you must be the new gal."

She drew up her chin. "I am Eliza O'Hanlan, the proprietress of this establishment for the time being. How may I assist you, gentlemen?"

The soldier laughed. "Propri-a-what?" He gave a whoop of laughter that made her wonder if he'd already been celebrating at the saloon. "Hey, Ed, you hear them fancy words she said?"

"I heard 'em." His friend chuckled. "I kinda liked it." He grabbed hold of her elbow. "What's your name, darlin'?"

"I am most certainly not your darlin' and my name is not your concern." She wrenched her arm away. "If you wish to…do business here this evening, you will unhand me and treat me with the proper respect due a lady."

"There she goes again," said the first man with a snicker.

Abraham loudly cleared his throat. Both soldiers glanced up at him as one of the girls—golden curls and an eager smile—Opal, perhaps?—rushed over and drew the attention of the gentlemen. "Come on boys, tell me who you're here to see—I sure hope it's me!"

And with that they followed her like a couple of ducklings.

Someone came up behind her. "I think the general idea is to make them feel welcome, not run them off."

Pulse racing at the deep, familiar voice, she turned

to face Doctor Sullivan. "I guess I need to work on my manners. Are you here this evening on business...or pleasure?"

One dark brow arched as though he found her question intriguing. "Actually, I'm here to check on your mother."

She frowned, catching sight of a large red stain on his shirt. "Is that blood?"

He glanced down. "Yes. Bad accident at the mill today. One of the workers cut off the fingers of his right hand."

"Is he..." A wave of nausea assailed her at the thought. "Going to be all right?"

The doctor gestured for her to precede him up the stairs. "If you mean will he survive, Miss O'Hanlan—"

"Eliza," she corrected.

Another raised brow. "Well, look who's making friends."

Her cheeks heated. "I...didn't mean to be so rude earlier. I was just taken aback by the methods used to...well, you understand." She glanced up at him and her stomach did a ridiculous little flip flop. He stopped, gazing at her, green eyes thoughtful.

She cleared her throat. "The gentleman who lost his fingers?"

"Right. Well, I'm hopeful he'll survive but that remains to be seen. He won't be able to work again anytime soon. If ever. Not too many jobs available for a mill foreman with only one good hand."

They had reached Adelaide's room and found her gazing at the door with interest. "Who lost his hand, Doc?" she asked as he breeched the door.

"Red McCleary," he said, waiting for Eliza to

follow him inside.

"No, oh that's awful." Adelaide shook her head. "And the missus with all them little ones about? 'Liza, talk to the girls in the morning, get them to fix up a basket with some food and see who can go over there to help them out over the next few days. They can take turns."

Eliza nearly choked. Her mother didn't actually mean... She turned a questioning gaze on the doctor.

"Your mother is quite a pillar of the community," he said, moving toward the bed and placing his bag on the nightstand. "During an influenza outbreak last winter, she and her girls nursed half the town back to health. I came down with it myself and was grateful for the help."

Addie waved a dismissive hand. "It weren't nothin'. We may be whores, but we're good neighbors is all."

"All right, Addie." The doctor lifted the covers to reveal the splintered appendage. "Let me take a look at this ankle."

Addie turned her painted gaze on Eliza as the doctor went about his examination. "'Liza Jane, why don't you ride out there with the doc tomorrow to check on Mrs. McCleary? I'm sure she'd appreciate a friendly vis—ow, Doc, that hurts."

Sullivan sat back with a grimace. "It's still pretty swollen. Are you staying off it? No walking around, no trying to go up and down the stairs?"

Addie pressed a hand to her heart. "Doc, I been an angel, I swear."

He propped another pillow under her lower leg. "Try to keep it elevated as much as possible, keep it up on pillows."

"Or fellows?" she cackled, but blanched when Eliza frowned at her.

"Speaking of fellows," he said, "I ran into Russ Holt this morning. I think he'd like to see you. Might do you both a world of good."

"He don't want to see me when I can't…" She let her words trail off, avoiding her daughter's gaze.

"Maybe that's not all he comes to see you for, Addie," he said and winked at her. "Ever think of that?"

He straightened and tucked his things back in the bag. "Miss Eliza, I'll be heading out to the McCleary place tomorrow morning bright and early. Be ready by seven if you care to ride along."

Chapter Six

The cooler air of morning was giving way to the heat of the day by the time the buggy pulled up at the McCleary residence.

Four young boys scampered out to meet them as Coyote pulled the wagon to a halt. Behind them came Mrs. McCleary. His stomach clenched at the sight of fresh bruises on her face.

Eliza shot him a questioning glance. He shook his head, silently beseeching her not to mention it. Red was a miserable son of a bitch. Coyote could only guess that the man had taken the frustration from his injuries out on his wife.

Ruby, who had been napping in the back of the wagon after a late night, sat up and stretched. "This where ya want me to stay and help, Doc?"

Mary McCleary stopped in her tracks.

Coyote turned to look behind him. Other than the bright red hair, without her fancy clothes and make up, Ruby looked like an ordinary girl.

Mary reached up to smooth back her riotous red curls. "Doc, we're good Christian people here. I don't think—"

"She's here to help with the boys and any chores you need done, Mary." Hesitation was evident on her face, but a light came into her eyes at the offer of assistance. Exhaustion weighed heavy on her features and he guessed with Red underfoot she hadn't gotten much rest. "She's not here to help with your husband in any capacity unless you are in the room."

Mary swallowed. "I—I don't know—"

Ignoring her hesitation, he turned and gestured toward Eliza, who looked as uncomfortable as Mary. "This is Miss O'Hanlan; she's Miss Adelaide's daughter."

The woman took a step back. "Oh, Lord, another one."

He raised his voice over her protests. "She's visiting from back east."

Eliza stepped forward, clutching the basket Aoife had filled as if it were a lifeline. "Mrs. McCarthy sent you cookies for the boys, biscuits and jam, some chicken soup, and her delicious canned peaches."

Mary's hand fluttered to her chest. "I—I don't know that I can accept charity—"

Coyote held the door open and gestured for the ladies to enter. "That's fine. Miss O'Hanlan can leave it on the table. If you don't want it, don't accept it."

They stepped into the tidy, sparsely furnished cabin.

"You look exhausted, Mrs. McCleary," Eliza said. "Why don't you sit and I'll make some coffee?"

Ruby nodded enthusiastically. "I'll bet them boys of yours would like som'a Aoife's biscuits and jam. Is it okay I give 'em some, Miz McCleary?"

Coyote left the three women to talk and entered the small room off the kitchen where Red slept.

The man rested with his head on the pillow, snoozing. Other than the sour smell of McCleary himself, no liquor odors permeated the room. Maybe he'd listened yesterday when Coyote had warned him to lay off the booze until he healed.

"How you feeling, Red?"

The man started and looked about before his gaze landed on his visitor. "I been better, Doc."

Coyote moved toward the bed. "I've come to take a look at that hand."

Bushy red eyebrows rose with interest. "I don't suppose you brought me anything for the pain?"

"Just Dover's Powder. I'll give you some now and leave the rest with Mary. She'll know when to give it to you."

The man grimaced and held up his wrapped hand. "I was hopin' for a bit of whiskey."

"That's the last thing you need right now." Coyote unwrapped the bandages, examining the injured nubs. The wound was ugly and raw. Corn meal had helped stop the bleeding yesterday, but it would be a miracle if infection didn't set in.

Red grimaced and cussed throughout the assessment. Finally, he called Mary in and with her help Coyote washed the digits, showing her how to clean, then rewrap them. She paled at the sight.

"You'll need to do this every day," he explained, though he already expected the worst. "At the first sign of infection or fever, you send one of the boys for me. Understand?"

The woman nodded, not making eye contact with him for longer than a scant second.

"I'll be by the day after tomorrow to check him again."

She nodded. "Thank you, Doc Sullivan."

Coyote waited while Mary gathered the discarded

wrappings and left the room. He stood in front of his patient.

"Miss Adelaide sent one of her girls here to help with the chores and the children so Mary can focus on you."

Red grunted.

"That's all she is here for." He looked into the other man's face, trying to read the stubborn expression. "She won't be coming into this room unless Mary needs her help."

He remained silent as he packed his things back into his bag, choosing his words carefully. "I'm leaving a weapon here with Ruby for protection. And when I come back, if I see fresh bruises on Mary or those boys, you and I are going to have a problem, do you understand?"

Red winced. "It's not what ya think, Doc. The woman…she asks for it, the way she runs her mouth. She goads me 'til I lose me temper."

"Stay in here and rest and let Mary do what she needs to do. And don't lose your temper again or you'll find out what happens when I lose mine." He turned to go, a knot twisting in his gut. As long as McCleary was bedridden it shouldn't be too hard on Mary, but once he was up and about…

Out in the kitchen, the women chatted over coffee. Coyote met Ruby's gaze. "When I come back, I'll bring one of the other girls to take your place. In the meantime, if anything comes up, or if there's any trouble, send one of the boys to town to find me."

She nodded. "We'll be fine, Doc. Don't you worry."

Mrs. McCleary didn't look so certain, studying

Ruby with a look of unease.

"Miss O'Hanlan?"

Eliza started as though deep in thought and the gaze she turned on him was filled with concern.

They said their goodbyes and headed out to the wagon. The boys, faces smeared with jam, followed as the wagon turned toward the road, waving until they were out of sight of the house.

Eliza turned in her seat. "That woman's face—"

He held up a hand. "I know what you're going to say."

"How can you—"

"McCleary is a mean son of a bitch, Miss Eliza, but you know the way of the world. There is only so much I can do." He tried to keep the hard edge of from his tone, but worry over what Red would put Mary through in the coming weeks weighed on him.

"So she has no choice but to…tolerate the beatings?" She folded her arms. "Is that what you mean by 'way of the world'?"

Her chin went up again. Dammit he knew that look. He slowed the wagon and urged the horses off to the side of the road. "What?"

"It just seems that you…as a doctor…isn't there something you could do?"

"As a doctor? No. As a man, I'd like to call him out and shoot him dead, but then what? How is Mary supposed to provide for those boys?" He sighed as the frustration he felt over the situation rose to the surface. "He drinks, he has a violent temper, and he beats his wife. I'm not sure what ivory tower you grew up in, Miss O'Hanlan, but here in the real world, life isn't fair, and it isn't easy."

She drew herself up straight. "Ivory tower? You mean caring for an old, bitter woman, my aunt, who loathed my very existence? Always forcing myself to be cheerful, always wanting to please her lest she put me out on the street? Is that the ivory tower to which you refer, Doctor Sullivan?"

"Don't go getting your feathers all ruffled, Eliza Jane, I was merely suggesting you've had a much different life than poor Mary McCleary."

"Don't you call me Eliza Jane." She folded her arms and faced the road. "Don't you dare."

He chuckled. "You've never been courted, have you?"

Her eyes widened. "Wh—what?"

He had to grin at her startled expression. "Your aunt was a spinster and so are you. I'll bet you've never even spoken to a man other than a doctor or preacher."

Her face went ghostly pale. "What kind of point are you trying to make with such nonsense?"

He slid closer to her in the seat. She scooted over but there was no farther to go without exiting the buggy. She was thinking about it though, from the way she kept looking from him to the ground and back again.

"The point that I've been wanting to kiss you since you stepped off that train."

"I hardly think this is the proper—"

"That's the problem." He hooked a hand behind her neck. "You think too much."

Before she could answer he pressed his lips to hers. She stiffened and he coaxed her lips with his, gently, so as not to spook her, until a small sigh escaped her and her lips softened.

The urge to deepen the kiss overcame him but he held back, knowing she would bolt like a startled doe if he did. But he lingered, acquainting himself with the taste of her, letting her get comfortable with him, before he pulled back to observe her reaction.

Satisfied, he slid back over in the seat, took up the reins and urged the horses forward, smiling that she remained silent for a moment.

****

Eliza's lips still tingled as the doctor finished his last stop of the morning. She had to resist the urge to press her fingertips to her mouth and savor the sensation.

Her first kiss! Oh, how many times she had closed her eyes and pressed her face to her pillow, imagining what it would be like to be kissed. Now at twenty-eight and quite overripe, she finally knew.

And it was better than she might have dreamed. The warmth of the doctor's lips on hers, the faint smell of coffee on his breath, the soft feel of his beard as it brushed her chin.

Heaven help her, she wanted to do it again.

She pressed a hand to her cheek, not at all surprised to find it flaming hot. Why, she was becoming as loose as the women at mother's establishment.

"You all right?"

Even his voice, that deep, rich baritone, had shivers moving over her in the heat of high noon.

"You look a little pink." He glanced skyward. "Gonna be a hot one today, we'd better get you out of this heat."

She fumbled with her hands in her lap. Being out here with him as he made his rounds of the town and the surrounding area was interesting. It was the most pleasant afternoon she'd had in some time. "I—I'm fine."

"I only have a couple more stops that I know of, but I'll make sure to get you back before the Social Club opens for business at two."

That was it? He had nothing to say about kissing her?

She sighed. The thought of entertaining and making small talk with a crowd of people again warred with her inclination to hide behind the drapes or sit quietly in a corner.

"Will you be by later? To check on mother, I mean." She wasn't sure which way to hope.

"Only if she needs me to. I want to ride out to the Holt ranch and check on that colt. And Russ." He looked behind them and then to the road ahead once more.

"You mentioned that name before. Who is he?"

"Well, Miss Eliza, he's your mother's gentleman friend, for lack of a better way to put it." He glanced over at her. "They've been not so secretly seeing one another for years."

"She never told me about him in her letters." She gazed down at the hands folded in her lap. There were so many things they had never talked about or shared. Certainly not like most mothers and daughters—then again, most mothers didn't own and operate a house of ill repute.

He gave a thoughtful sigh. "I don't think Addie realizes herself that she cares for him. She's had a hard life, your mother. Coming out here with that worthless Farley Willowby only to get stuck with his debts and his run-down bordello when he died. A weaker woman would have crumbled, but not Adelaide."

"I...I didn't know that. About the debts and the run-down business. I was just a child when she left. I only knew that she promised to come back for me and never did."

He glanced over at her. "The Social Club wasn't always the clean, well-run establishment it is now. Not the sort of place to raise a child."

A hot ball of emotion lodged in her throat. Tears threatened and she blinked them back. "How do you know my mother so well?"

"Not the way you think," he said, his tone silken smooth. "But I know Aoife and she's given me an ear full on more than one occasion."

Eliza tried to make sense of it all. "I see."

She started when the warmth of his hand covered hers. "Give her a chance, Miss Eliza. Stay long enough to get acquainted with your mother. It won't give you back the years you've lost, but there's still time for the two of you to get to know one another."

"The train doesn't come until Sunday anyway." She pulled in a shaky breath, looking down at his hand on hers, then back to his face. "I'll see how I feel about things by then."

Up ahead was a small cabin, and like many others they had visited today, a white cloth hung from the window. She'd learned this indicated the occupants had need for the doctor to stop. She sighed as he steered the buggy toward the road leading to the house.

She had five days left here in town to decide what to do.

She wondered if she could get him to kiss her again

before the train arrived.

Chapter Seven

Coyote rested with his arms on the fence, watching the young colt he'd delivered a couple of days ago prance around with its mother. Russ and Caleb Holt stood nearby. He'd come to inquire about a horse, but this little one, with her reddish gold coat and white streak on her nose, had somehow managed to capture his heart.

"You delivered her," Caleb said. "You get to name her."

"E.J." The words were out before he could even think about it. For Eliza Jane. He shook his head. Dammit, he had never let a woman get into his head so easily before. But this one…he'd tasted her sweet lips and he already wanted more than that.

"Those initials belong to anyone I know?" Russ asked with a sly grin.

"Nope." Coyote kept his gaze straight ahead. "Just thought it suited her."

"How's she settling in over there?" Russ looked back to the horse. "Poor girl. I've been telling Addie for years no good would come of keeping her business a secret. Had to be a hell of a shock."

"It was," Coyote sighed. "But you and Eef were right to tell me to send for her. She and Addie need to get to know each other. And Eliza is almost as stubborn as her mother. If I can get her to stay a while, maybe that ankle of Addie's will finally heal."

The older man chuckled. "I never met a more stubborn woman in my life than Adelaide Willowby."

Coyote tore his gaze from the horse and turned to look at Russ. "Then I'll have to introduce you to her daughter. She sure was curious about you."

Russ blanched. "Doc, you know Adelaide doesn't like folks knowing her private business. Ain't me whose gonna do any talkin'."

Coyote laughed. "Every soul in town knows about the two of you."

The gray handlebar mustache twitched as Russ grinned. "I thought you came here to talk about horses, not my love life. Docs are supposed to keep things about patients confidential-like."

Coyote took the hint. "That I did. Caleb, let's talk about this little one."

"Yes, sir." Caleb clapped him on the shoulder. "Come on up to the house. I've got some new cigars from back east. I think you'll like them."

Russ straightened and pushed away from the fence. "And I could use a drink."

Coyote shook his head. "I keep telling you, Russ. That stuff'll kill ya."

The older man grinned. "Then at least I know how I'll go."

****

Eliza stood back and watched Adelaide in her element. With the help of the bouncer, Abraham, who carried her down the stairs this evening, her mother held court once again.

Sitting on the bench beside the pianist, she sang, throwing her arms out wide and shimmying, then launched into a series of off-color stories and jokes. The men waiting their turn for the girl of their choice threw their heads back in laughter. Finally, Abraham lifted her so she could sit on the piano with her ankle propped on a pillow, singing what Eliza could only guess were saloon songs.

The male clientele hooted and applauded; Adelaide had them in the palm of her hand. Eliza kept a close eye on the door and as one man after another was called by the girl of his choice, she made sure he had a fresh drink in his hand.

She measured the drops carefully and kept the drinks separate. Smaller men got less of the elixir; she kept those drinks on the tray to her left. The larger men's drinks got more drops and those were on her right. Each of the girls had a small vial with extra "medicine" tucked into her bosom in case more was needed to accomplish the goal.

She still didn't approve of this whole sordid idea, but for now she was left with no choice but to help. The thought of being an accomplice to this ill-thought-out venture nagged at her.

There were also drinks available for the men that the girls didn't want drugged, the clients they actually wanted to entertain. This was communicated to her by a wink from one of the girls and a wisecrack about not making his drink too strong so that he would be able to "go all night."

What happened once they were upstairs and behind closed doors was a bit of a mystery. Eliza understood the potion only knocked them out for a little while, and the girls stayed with them and slipped back into the bed as they woke. They were fed stories, she supposed, about their prowess and stamina before being sent on their way.

And then the next man took his turn.

She had thought a great deal about what the doctor said—about her mother struggling to make a run-down establishment successful. She didn't necessarily agree with the way Mother went about it, but it did cause her to study Adelaide in a new light. Business woman. Someone of strength and drive.

Eliza had been just a tot when Adelaide had married the smooth-talking Mr. Willowby. She didn't recall much about her stepfather but Aunt Cornelia certainly had a good deal to say about him over the years. None of it good. Her own father had died before she was born. Adelaide had met him, married him and buried him all in the space of a year, she'd once said.

Aoife came up to stand beside her. "She's overdoing it. She'll be exhausted come morning."

By now Eliza had learned that the woman's tut-tutting, though it sounded brusque, was simply her way of showing concern. "If she's tired tomorrow maybe she'll rest. This has been good for her. She needs to be around people, not cooped up in that room all day."

"It was a wonderful idea," the Irishwoman said. "I'm ashamed I never thought of it m'self. Maybe we can bring her down tomorrow to sit in the garden or on the porch."

"I think she'd like that." Eliza agreed. "I think the less she stays hidden away the happier she will be." As long as they kept her foot propped up it should be all right. Still, she would have to check with the doctor about that. For some reason a little thrill rushed over her. A legitimate excuse to see him again. She pressed a finger to her lips as the memory of kissing him stole over her once more. She hadn't stopped thinking of him since that kiss, the memory of it stole over her at odd moments.

"Git!" Aoife shooed a soldier who stumbled and weaved a little too close to them, eyeing Eliza like the last slice of pie. "Off ya go, or I'll have Abraham show ya the door."

****

Long after night had fallen, Eliza stood in Miss Addie's elaborate pink room, helping her get ready for bed.

"I ain't tired yet," her mother protested, even as she stifled a yawn. "I don't go to bed much before dawn— someone…" She yawned again. "Someone's gotta entertain the men while they're waiting…"

Eliza tucked a pillow under mother's foot and tugged the covers up over her, not giving her a choice. "Amethyst and Emerald are down there, can't you hear them singing?"

Miss Addie's eyes were already drifting closed. "I can't thank you enough, 'Liza Jane. It felt so doggone good to get outta this room."

Eliza patted her hand. "I'll have Abraham bring you down for a while tomorrow afternoon, but you have to promise me you'll rest until then. No trying to get up on your own."

Addie yawned again and nodded.

"We need to talk about your bookkeeping tomorrow. I've been over the ledgers and I can't make heads or tails of your figures," Eliza added. She'd spent a few hours trying to understand the lack of organization in her mother's books.

"Ain't no one ever complained about my figure before," Addie said with that now familiar glint in her eyes.

At Eliza's stern look, Mother waved a dismissive hand. "They make sense enough."

"Not for me." Eliza leaned in to press a kiss to her mother's forehead.

Adelaide grabbed her hand. "It means the world to me, you bein' here you know." Tears welled in her blue eyes. "I thought if you knew, you'd hate me."

Eliza patted the hand that held hers, but mother still didn't let go. Unable to move away, she sat on the bedside. "I don't hate you. I admit I have been hurt and angry at times to think you never sent for me, but Coyo—Doctor Sullivan helped me to understand things a little better."

"Coyote, is it?" Adelaide grinned. "I suppose you might have noticed he's handsome, too."

Eliza looked away as heat poured into her cheeks.

Addie gave a whoop of laughter. "He's a mighty good catch, Eliza Jane."

At last, her mother released her hand, and Eliza rose, smoothing the coverlet and tucking it around the tiny form. "I'm sure I wouldn't know what to do with him if I caught him."

"Well now, that's something your mama could help you with, you know." Addie's gaze met hers. "What to do with a man after ya caught him."

Her cheeks were scorching hot now. "Mother!"

"Well, it ain't all about the sex, you know. Ya gotta stroke their egos, *and* their—"

"*Mother!*"

Addie laughed. "I left you with your Aunt Cornelia

too long. You're all prim and fussy, just like her."

"We can talk more in the morning." Eliza leaned in to kiss her cheek once more.

"Will you have breakfast with me up here? I'd like that a lot. We got so much catching up to do." Addie's eyes were hopeful.

"Apparently so. You can tell me all about your paramour over breakfast."

"My para *what*?"

"Mr. Holt. Doctor Sullivan tells me you two are…very well acquainted."

Addie's head dropped back onto the pillow. "As soon as this ankle heals, I'm gonna give that Coyote a swift kick in the ass."

Chapter Eight

The sun was just beginning to peek over the mountains when Coyote stepped outside onto the porch. The chirping of the birds and the smell of pine greeted him as he lifted a steaming cup of coffee to his lips. The first sip was still on his tongue when he noticed a commotion from up the street.

The commotion was actually one of the McCleary boys, if the red hair was any indication, running hell-bent for leather down the street. From this distance he couldn't tell which one it was, but it looked too small to be the oldest and too big to be the youngest.

He'd just set his cup down when young Daniel McCleary clambered up the porch steps.

"Whoa," he caught the child by the shoulders, worried momentum would carry him into the wall. "Slow down, son."

The boy's chest heaved with exertion. "Doc, ya gotta come quick."

"Get your breath. Whatever it is, I can't help if you pass out." He kept his tone calm, hoping it would relax the boy a bit.

Daniel bent at the waist and took a few deep gulps of air. Finally, he straightened. "It's Pa. You gotta come."

A weight settled in Coyote's gut. He'd worried about infection setting in. "Wait here. I'll get my bag. Is he feverish?"

"No, he ain't got a fever, Doc." Wide, frightened eyes met his. "He's dead."

****

Coyote looked from the corpse of Redmond McCleary to the two ladies in the barn with him. Experience told him the man had been dead for close to a day, not just a few hours, as Ruby and Mary insisted.

Something wasn't right.

"Who brought him out to the barn?" he asked.

"I did." Ruby hugged her arms about herself, eyeing the body as if afraid it would come back to life at any second. "I drug him out here early this mornin'."

"Mary," he said, turning to Mrs. McCleary. "Tell me again what happened."

The new widow winced, then glanced at the ground. "He...he was cleaning his revolver and it musta gone off."

"With his left hand?" Coyote pressed.

It didn't make sense that a man who was right-handed would take it upon himself to clean his gun with his non-dominant hand the day after such an accident. It would be months, years even before he would have the dexterity needed in that hand for even minor tasks.

"I...I guess." Mary glanced from the remains of her husband back to the house. "Can you cover him back up Doc? I don't want the boys to see."

"And this happened early this morning?" He folded his arms and turned his gaze on Ruby. "So Red was cleaning his gun before daybreak?"

"I...I gotta check on the boys." Mary scampered off like a scared rabbit.

"I'll go with ya," Ruby offered.

Coyote took hold of the girl's arm as she went past, stopping her. "I've seen a lot of gun-cleaning injuries in my time," he said when she gazed at him wide-eyed. "Never one square in the chest like that."

"Really?" The girl gave a nervous laugh. "How 'bout that."

"Mary's lip wasn't swollen when I saw her yesterday." He placed his hands to his hips. "I don't care which one of you did it, and I'll do my best to convince the sheriff this was an accident. But you need to come up with a story that makes more sense and stop acting guilty or Earl will lock up the both of you."

"We don't know who done it, Doc," she whispered, her eyes welling with tears. "He was knockin' her around again last night. I did what I could to stop him." She rolled up her sleeve to show him the finger-shaped bruises on her arm. "He grabbed me and flung me against the wall. He was gonna beat me, too."

"Was he drinking?"

"No, that's what set him off, Mary dumped all the liquor. This is why Miss Addie uses the medicine, you know." She gestured toward the body. "Men like him."

"I know." He nodded. "It's okay. What happened next?"

"Mary came outside—I was trying to clean her face up. And then we heard the shot." She trembled. "All four boys was in the house; we thought the worst. Then they come out and said their Pa was dead and they weren't tellin' who done it."

Coyote raked a hand through his hair. "Jesus." No wonder they were both so nervous.

Ruby's eyes welled with tears. "She'll go to jail— for that matter so will I—'fore we let anything happen to them boys."

"No one's going to jail, Ruby." He heaved a sigh as an idea formed in his mind. "You have my word on that."

****

The breakfast table the next morning buzzed with speculation about who had shot whom.

"What is this about a shooting?" Eliza asked, taking a seat at the table while waiting for Aoife to prepare Adelaide's breakfast.

The kitchen door was propped open to catch the cooler morning air. The squawk and cluck of chickens as well as a rooster who crowed at all hours carried over the conversation. A bowl of fresh eggs sat on the table, and the smell of apples and cinnamon drifted from the pie safe. Aoife had certainly been up and about early.

The older woman set two cups of coffee on a tray before her along with a pitcher of cream. "The McCleary residence."

An image of the battered wife and four young boys leapt to mind. "My God. Mary?"

"It weren't Mary," spoke up Emerald, her jewel green gaze intent on Eliza. "It were the mister."

Amethyst went slack-jawed at the information. "The one what got his fingers cut off?"

The other girl nodded.

"Do we know what happened?" Eliza asked, liberally buttering two slices of toast and placing them on the tray.

Aoife sank into a chair opposite her. "Not yet. Doc says Ruby is going to be there another day or so to help. Mary must be in a terrible state, poor woman."

"We should take a ride out there, Auntie Aoife. See if she needs anything."

"A man's what she'll be needin'," Aoife insisted. "How is she supposed to raise four boys with no husband to provide?"

Eliza bit her lip, a bit unnerved by the whole thing. "There must be someplace she could go, or a job she could do. Something besides the obvious."

"You mean besides layin' on her back in a place like this?" Aoife tut-tutted as she rose and returned to the stove.

Emerald raised her chin. "I'm grateful to Miss Addie that I don't have to do that. Unless I choose to."

Amethyst nudged her in the ribs. "You only *choose to* with Abraham."

Emerald's cheeks went bright pink. "Amethyst!"

Eliza listened to the banter, marveling at the great affection between the girls. How on earth could they speak of such things so casually?

"Oh, it's no big secret, we all know how you two get on." She looked at her friend, then sobered. "Me too. It weren't like that the other places I've worked either. How'd you avoid it, Aoife? You were widowed young."

Aoife stood and moved toward the stove. "For one thing, I didn't have children like poor Mary. Adelaide came to visit me after my Paddy died in the minin' accident. She was very kind to me, bringin' me food and what-not and some of her girls to look after me. I'd like to have never got out of bed again if it weren't for Addie and those girls."

"Crystal and me," Pearl spoke up. She'd been so quiet, Eliza had barely noticed her standing in the corner by the pie safe, enjoying the air from the open door. "I remember that."

"Who is Crystal?" Eliza asked, confused at this new name.

"Never you mind her." Aoife crossed herself with great reverence. "God rest her soul."

The other girls crossed themselves as well. Eliza wondered if they were Catholic, too, or simply following Aoife's example.

Pearl picked up the coffee pot to refill her cup. "Tell the rest, Eef."

"Oh, it's silly." Aoife began to crack eggs into a bowl with one hand, dropping the shells aside.

"She baked her way in to this job," Pearl said with a laugh. "Ol' Farley couldn't resist her sugar cookies."

Aoife looked thoughtful as she used the wooden whisk. "I wanted to return her kindness so I sent her some baked goods. As it turned out, Mr. Willowby had quite the sweet tooth and the cook they had at that time was not to his likin'. So they offered me a job."

Emerald shook her head. "You got lucky."

"Maybe I did at that." The eggs sizzled as the Irishwoman poured them into a pan. "I hope Mary McCleary does, as well. Four mouths to feed as well as her own. Poor thing."

"Can we ask Mrs. Lowery if she needs help?" Amethyst took a bite of toast dripping with honey, wiping her chin with the back of her hand. "We're some of her best customers. No one wears fancier dresses than us."

"That miserable woman," Aoife grumbled from her post at the stove.

"Who is that?" Eliza asked, wondering at Aoife's

apparent distaste of the woman.

"She owns the Lowery Dress Shoppe in town." Emerald sat up straighter. "In fact I'd wager if Miss Addie asked her, the ol' witch would trip over herself to oblige."

Aoife shook her head and pulled the pan from the heat. "Well, Adelaide's in no shape to go out, and we certainly can't ask the Widow Lowery to come here."

"Then we need to pay her a call," Eliza said, spooning a pile of fluffy eggs onto a plate for her mother.

The two girls at the table stared at her with stunned expressions.

She shrugged. "Perhaps it's time Miss Adelaide's daughter ordered a few dresses."

****

Tingles of excitement danced over Eliza as the carriage bounced along the streets of Wylder. For the first time, she was really getting a look at the heart of the town.

Aoife had insisted the driver take the long way around so Eliza could get a full view.

The carriage traveled down Buckboard Alley, past the bakery and the boarding house the doctor had mentioned.

"Everyone here is so friendly," Eliza mused as yet another man stopped in the street, smiled and raised his hat.

Aoife was quick to snap the curtain closed. "Just remember whose carriage you're ridin' in." The older woman sat back in her seat, mouth set in a frown. "They're not bein' friendly in the way ya think."

Eliza opened the window covering just enough to

see out as the carriage passed the newspaper office and the grand Wylder Hotel. On the other side of the street was the Wylder Mercantile. Eliza angled her head even as the horse clip-clopped past, trying to get a look at the goods on display.

On the corner of Wylder Street and Sidewinder Lane was a simple white house, nestled between the telegraph office and the apothecary. A small inviting porch held a single rocking chair and a sign overhead simply read "Doctor."

Eliza turned in her seat, staring after it as the carriage pulled up in front of Lowery's Dress Shoppe.

Aoife chuckled knowingly. "Something catch your eye back there, did it?"

Heat rose in Eliza's cheeks. "I never thought about where he lived."

They climbed out of the carriage and up the few steps to the dress shop.

Eliza couldn't help a small cry of pleasure at the beautiful creations and fabrics surrounding her as they walked in.

A plump, gray-haired woman appeared at the counter, peering over her spectacles. "May I help you?"

Aoife offered a curt nod. "This is Adelaide Willowby's daughter, Eliza. She's come to see about ordering dresses."

The woman's hand fluttered to her throat to fiddle with the brooch there. "I see."

"Adelaide's *daughter*," Aoife emphasized.

Eliza stepped away from the fabric to approach the counter, offering her most pleasant smile. "I'm sure I won't need anything elaborate. Just a few new things."

The woman's shoulders relaxed a bit as she studied

her.

"I'll need them shipped to New York, of course. I'm only here to help until Mother is back on her feet again." She fingered a sample of fabric on display, rubbing the velvety texture between her fingers, surprised at the choices available in a small western town.

The woman's eyes sparkled with interest. "New York? Well, I should think the fancier materials, then."

From the corner of her eye, Eliza spotted a little room off to one side of the shop where a young woman sat at a sewing machine. Aoife walked toward it and poked her head in to say hello.

Mrs. Lowery cast a sharp glance their direction.

"Yes, New York," Eliza spoke up, drawing the woman's attention back to her. "The theater, the opera, the museums. I do so miss it." When was the last time she had actually been to any of those? Aunt Cornelia wasn't much for going out. But she sensed the dress shop owner and Aoife didn't really like each other, so best to keep her occupied.

The woman's gaze returned to her. "Now about those dresses…"

For the next hour Eliza kept the woman busy with patterns and fabrics. Only after she had ordered half a dozen dresses with matching hats did she mention the newly widowed Mary McCleary and inquire if there was a way she could be of help.

"I already have one widow working for me," Mrs. Lowery snapped. "I can't be expected to provide employment for every woman in town who loses her husband. I lost my own, some years back, but I worked hard to keep this shop. Women gotta learn to find their way, you know."

"Of course," Eliza agreed. "I just thought that since you take in laundry and mending you might need someone to help with the sewing or ironing."

Her hand fluttered to the brooch at her neck again. "Well, I just don't know…"

"Did I tell you mother is planning to visit me in New York next spring?" She gave the shop owner a decidedly sweet smile. "I can't wait to introduce her to all the wonderful dress shops, I just know she'll come back with an entire wardrobe of clothes."

Mrs. Lowery's sharp gaze narrowed. "I'm sure I could use help with the ironing, but those four hellions of hers had better stay out of my shop," she spoke through gritted teeth. "I don't need those wild boys tracking up the store and touching the linens."

"Oh, how very kind of you, Mrs. Lowery." Eliza squeezed her hand. "When Mary is ready, I'll have her stop in and see you."

"The back door," the woman growled. "I don't need people seeing a filthy Irish immigrant at my front door. I could lose customers."

Outside in the carriage, Eliza sagged in exhaustion. "My word, what a hateful woman."

"Filthy Irish immigrant indeed," Aoife spat. "A widow herself, she is, you think she'd be more charitable and not such a hypocrite."

"Yes," Eliza agreed. "The seamstress seems very nice though."

"Laurel," Aoife said. "And Leona does the washin'. She works those poor girls like slaves. Miserable old woman. And Laurel has the most darling little boy. Such a sweet girl. Her husband got gold fever and up and left her, don't you know. Poor thing."

The carriage lurched forward and Eliza couldn't resist turning in her seat for another look at the town. "I just ordered six dresses I'll probably never wear except to the market or library. But if it helps poor Mrs. McCleary, I guess it was worth it."

"This is true," Aoife said with a sigh. "By the by, I didn't know you were such a fan of the opera."

Eliza glanced over at her and giggled. "Actually, I've never been in my life."

****

Coyote sat across from the sheriff, trying hard to maintain eye contact. Earl Hanson drummed his fingers on the desk, studying him intently.

"So let me see if I understand this. A man who just lost all the fingers on his right hand—a right-handed man at that? He chooses the day after to clean his revolver." The older man scratched his bald head. "He don't check to see if it's loaded first. And then it goes off and hits him dead center in the chest?"

The key to any good story was believing it yourself. Coyote rested his ankle on one knee, trying to appear relaxed and comfortable. "Come on, Earl. You can guess how it really happened. Who knows how much McCleary had to drink, or what was going through his head. He was never going to have a job again, he had to know it."

"But if you're cleaning your revolver and you got it in your lap…" he moved his hand from his lap to his chin, demonstrating. "I'm not thinking you'd shoot yourself in the chest."

"I examined the body myself and that's where the kill shot hit." Coyote nodded, sticking to the truth as much as possible.

Hanson tugged at his long, well-groomed mustache, a sure sign the gears were turning in the lawman's head. "Everyone knows how he knocked that woman around. You don't think she'd…"

Coyote swallowed. It wouldn't be easy to steer the old hound off the scent, but he'd be damned if anyone hanged for this. "I don't think she has it in her. Mary's afraid of her own shadow. In spite of how poorly he treated her, she's no killer."

The other man continued to pull at his mustache.

Coyote shifted, stretching an arm along the back of the chair. "No one is going to miss the likes of Red McCleary. However he managed to do it, he did this town a favor."

Earl started, as if he'd forgotten anyone else was there. "I ain't sayin' that's not true Doc, but I'd like to take a look at the body myself, just to be sure."

"You sure about that? Gus already picked him up for burial, but if you want to take a look, we can head over there. Just remember, McCleary's been dead for two days in this heat, so you'll want to bring a handkerchief." He gestured toward his nose. "Some oil of peppermint might help, too."

The sheriff's sun-reddened face paled.

"He took his own life, Earl. Mary would never admit he killed himself, you know how the Papists are about these things."

"How's that?" The sheriff eased to his feet stiffly and headed for a file drawer, wincing as he moved.

"They can't bury their dead in the Catholic cemetery if they die by suicide." Coyoted explained.

Earl grunted, shuffling through papers.

"So you can see why she's insisting it was accidental." Coyote settled into the story now that he'd put the idea into the sheriff's mind. "What are you going to see from looking at the body that I haven't already?"

The man's weary gaze met his. He tossed a stack of papers bound with twine onto his desk. "That right there? That's a list of complaints about Red McCleary. Everyone from Sonny Cash and the girls over at the saloon, to Miss Adelaide, the Holts, and men he worked with up at the mill. Any one of those folks could'a wanted him dead bad enough to do somethin' about it."

"Maybe, but Red did it for them. Let the woman bury her husband, Earl." Coyote shook his head. "Hasn't she been through enough?"

The sheriff pushed the drawer closed and walked slowly back toward his desk, favoring one knee the whole way. "You'll give me your word there was no foul play involved?"

A wave of relief washed over him. "I didn't see anything that made me think that." He leaned forward in the chair. "Now then, how's that gout?"

Chapter Nine

"You spend far too much money on alcohol." Seated in comfortable chairs in the garden with a gentle breeze stirring an otherwise hot afternoon, Eliza faced her mother.

Adelaide, bad leg propped on a stool and pillows, pulled a face. "It ain't important."

Eliza lifted the tea pot Aoife had thoughtfully provided and poured them each a cup. "I would argue it is." She leaned over to hand a saucer and a couple of freshly baked molasses cookies to her mother.

"You know why we need the booze, it's to hide the taste of the medicine."

Eliza glanced down at the ledger in her lap. "Why so much?"

"It ain't all booze. The liquor expenses I mean." Adelaide nibbled at one of the cookies. "I can't have folks knowin' about the medicine so I hide the cost of it in the liquor expenses."

"Oh, dear God." Eliza rubbed fingertips over her forehead. "You can't do—"

Her mother studied her closer. "You look so much like your daddy when you do that."

"You're changing the subject." Still, the words got her thinking. She had wondered about him her entire life. "What was he like?"

"You." Adelaide laughed. "Tall and thin. Your blue eyes, that's from me, but your hair color and stubborn nature? That's all John." She reached for her teacup. "Lordy, I loved that man. Met him when I was sixteen, married him when I was seventeen, buried him when I was eighteen."

Eliza leaned to refill her mother's cup. "How did he die?"

"Fever. It came on sudden, and just like that he was gone. I got sick, too. I was already expectin' you and until you were born, we didn't know..." Her eyes welled and she dabbed at them with a napkin. "If you'd be all right."

Aunt Cornelia had never told her any of this.

Adelaide sniffled. "He was so excited to meet you. Used to put his hand on my belly all the time and talk to you. And you'd kick right back."

A lump welled in Eliza's throat. She had pined much of her life for the father she'd never known. "You lost him, you lost Mister Willowby, that's a lot on someone so young."

"Farley Willowby wasn't worth the salt in my tears," Adelaide growled. "And I never shed a single drop over that man. He was a liar and a cheat and I was naïve and desperate. When he died, he left me penniless and in debt up to my eyeballs."

"I'm sorry, Mama. You must have worked very hard to overcome all of that." Eliza lightened her tone.

"I married once for love, and once for money," Adelaide sighed. "Got cheated both times. I'm not complainin', though. I learned a lot along the way. It made me a survivor." She took a sip of her tea. "I don't have to rely on or answer to any man. That's what I want for you, Eliza Jane."

"There's no worry about that, I'm quite the spinster."

Addie shrugged. "You don't have to be."

Eliza released a huff of frustration. "If you are implying what I think you are…"

"Well now, Coyote is single, too—"

Heat scorched her cheeks. "Well, maybe there's a reason for that, maybe he's sloppy or cantankerous, or—"

"Widowed." Adelaide said. "She died during childbirth while he was off at war."

"I see." Questions began to roll through her mind. She had never imagined him as married or having children. What a terrible thing to lose a wife and child like that.

"There's somethin' else you should know," her mother added.

Oh Lord, more? "Yes?"

"The girl I told you about. The one I was so close to that I lost? She—"

"What's all this boo-hooin' I hear?" The deep gravely voice started them both.

Eliza started as a tall, gray-haired man loped into the garden. He pulled his hat from his head, revealing shoulder length silver hair.

"Oh, Russ," Adelaide wailed, adjusting her blouse and fluffing her hair. "I told you I wasn't fit for company these days!"

His face lit up at the sight of her mother. "You look good to me. A sight for *real* sore eyes."

He turned to Eliza, as if just noticing her. "Well look at you," he said, face breaking into a warm smile.

"You must be Eliza Jane."

She stood to greet him, her hand dwarfed as both his large hands covered it. He squeezed tight and she felt immediately at ease. "Mother, where have you been hiding this handsome gentleman?"

He chuckled. "I like this girl already."

She invited him to have a seat and handed him a cup of tea and a saucer of cookies. The cup looked small and awkward in his large hands, but he held it up with a smile. "Can't remember the last time I had a cup of tea."

"*Hmph*. You and Aoife drink plenty of tea—you just don't use cream and sugar," Addie scolded. "As if you need to do more drinkin'."

"Mother, do I detect a note of jealousy?"

Addie waved a dismissive hand. "No, those two just get into mischief when they get their heads together, is all. Like haulin' my daughter clear across the country to take care of me when I'm perfectly capa—"

Russ set his cup aside and strode over to plant a kiss on Addie's forehead. "You fuss worse than an old wash woman, anyone ever tell you that?"

Mother's cheeks glowed pink. "Just you, Cowboy."

Rather than feeling uncomfortable at the display of affection, Eliza was charmed. Clearly these two were as much in love as Coyote suggested. It warmed her heart to think Mother had someone who genuinely cared for her, in spite of what she did for a living.

She had always hoped that one day she would have something similar. But she would be returning to New York soon, and taking any hope of finding love with her.

The thought left a hollow feeling in her stomach.

Russ eased back into his chair. "That's a long face if ever I saw one."

"Just gathering wool, I suppose." She glanced back down at the ledgers in hand. "Why don't I leave the two of you alone for now? We can finish talking about the numbers later."

"Or not," Addie piped up over the rim of her teacup. "Ain't really much to discuss, Eliza Jane. They are what they are."

"And they're a mess," Eliza sing-songed back.

Russ hooted with laughter. "Adelaide Willowby, I think you've met your match."

****

The afternoon shadows had grown long by the time Coyote headed toward the Wylder Mercantile. After a long day of tending the very sick, the very old, and the very young—he'd delivered a baby a few hours ago—he was ready to head home. As soon as he checked on Miss Adelaide at the Social Club.

But first he needed to restock some supplies before Finn Wylder closed for the night. As he approached the mercantile, he noticed Ezra Barlow slumped in a chair on the porch, hat pulled down to shade his face from the late afternoon sun.

Coyote hadn't seen him since he'd chased him away from Eliza her first day in town. He probably should apologize for threatening to shoot the young man. As he walked past, he heard a loud guttural snore from Ezra's direction. Well, another time then.

The bell over the door gave a merry jingle as he pushed it open. Finn Wylder looked up in greeting, his expression a bit flustered. "Doc, what brings you in today?"

A glance around showed one of the ladies from town, as well as Ruby, the youngest McCleary boy, and Eliza, all standing together in the middle of the store. For a moment, he stood to drink in the sight of her. The collar of her blue dress was buttoned up to her throat but it brought out the magnificent blue of her eyes. He took in her soft, pink lips, reliving the stolen kiss from yesterday.

"I think it's a disgrace." The voice of Una Barlow, Ezra's mother, brought him out of his reverie. "Lord knows what that child is exposed to running about with the likes of you."

"I only brung him in for a peppermint stick, Miz Barlow," Ruby explained.

"I'll thank you to keep your judgmental, sanctimonious opinion to yourself." Eliza sounded cool and composed but he noticed she squeezed the basket in her hand so hard her knuckles were white.

"Ladies," Finn's voice rose above the commotion. "Can we please just get on with our business? The store closes at five." He glanced at Coyote and rolled his eyes.

Coyote removed his hat, smoothing a hand over his hair. "Afternoon, Mrs. Barlow."

Una didn't acknowledge the greeting. "No child should be running about in the company of a harlot!"

Ruby placed her hands over the boy's ears. "Miz Barlow, not in front of the boy!"

Eliza stepped forward, placing herself between the two women. "How dare you call her that?"

The older woman's eyes narrowed. "You, a Jezebel's daughter, have no right to scold me. Why that mother of yours—"

"Ladies, ladies," Finn called again.

Both of Una's chins came up whiplash fast. "There is only one *lady* present, sir."

Coyote stepped closer, intent on diffusing the situation. "What seems to be the trouble here?"

Mrs. Barlow, happiest when finding fault with others, barely glanced in his direction. "I was just telling Mr. Wylder I should not have to shop in a store with these....*women*."

"Wylder's Mercantile is the only store in town, Una," Coyote pointed out. "Cheyenne's what, fifteen miles away? That's a mighty long ride."

The plump widow drew herself up straighter, gaze narrowed on the women before her. "If he won't toss them out, then perhaps I should take my business there."

"Now, Una," Coyote said, adopting the gentle tone he used when tending an injured child or animal. "I'm sure you don't want to go that far for sugar and flour."

His gaze met Eliza's. Her cheeks blushed to the enticing pink he'd noticed after their kiss. Was it from the heated exchange with the self-righteous Mrs. Barlow, or was she was remembering their kiss? And like him, hoping to do it again...

Una was in her element now, it seemed, spitting venom, eyes blazing with indignation. "It's preferable to being in the same room with *soiled women*."

Coyote folded his arms. "Ma'am, that's not a very Christian thing to say."

"Really?" Icicles all but dripped from her voice. "And when was the last time you darkened the doorway of a church, Doctor?"

"I'm busy doing the Lord's work in my own way, Una. People do get sick on Sundays." He dug in his pocket for a coin and placed it on the counter. "Finn, let me pay for young Malachy's candy—and one for each of his brothers."

"That's might kind'a ya, Doc." Ruby tousled the child's red curls. "It's been a rough coupl'a days on them boys." She took Malachy's hand and led him over to the counter where brightly colored candy sticks were displayed in glass jars.

Coyote caught Una's arctic stare as it swung back his direction. "You did hear about Mary McCleary's husband passing away?"

Her gaze darted to the boy, who leaned up on his tiptoes to show Finn which treat he wanted. For once, it seemed she chose not to speak her mind. "Yes. Of course."

Eliza shifted the basket to her other arm. "I'm sure the ladies' auxiliary is preparing baskets of food and supplies, since that's the *Christian* thing to do."

"She's a Papist," the woman said through pinched lips. "Perhaps the women of *her* church should do so."

Ruby walked past, followed by young Malachy, who skipped along behind her, his delighted gaze never leaving the candy stick in his hand.

The bell over the door rang and Ezra Barlow stepped inside. "Ma, what's taking so long?" His gaze swept over the ladies assembled and his ears turned a bright scarlet.

"Well, if you change your mind about that charity basket, Mrs. Barlow, you can always tell Ezra." Eliza took her purchases from the counter and placed them in the basket on her arm. "He can pass the message along to Ruby the next time he comes to pay a visit." She gave the woman a charming smile. "She's his favorite, you know."

Regal as a queen, she swept past without looking over her shoulder. At the door she paused. "Afternoon, Ezra. I assume we'll see you at the usual time tonight?"

Chapter Ten

Aoife stood scrubbing dishes at the kitchen sink, her hands red from the hot dishwater. "Now, girl, you don't want to go around rufflin' *those* particular feathers."

Eliza folded her arms and leaned against the nearby table. "What a horrible woman. She doesn't scare me in the least."

"She and that Mildred Lowery are the worst gossips in Wylder. Tweak Una's nose too many times and you'll find yourself the victim of some nasty rumors." She gestured for Eliza to move aside, then reached for the kettle of water she'd set to boil. "Take it from someone who knows."

Steam rose as the water filled the pan in the sink and Aoife added a few pumps of water to it. "Are you saying she's done this before?"

"Oh yes. To me, to your mother. And countless other women in town." She nodded. "Uppity, thinks the only God that counts is the one in her church. Her and that awful Mildred Lowery are tighter than the knots in a quilting circle. They take after anyone who gets up their ire."

Eliza grinned at the way the word came out with Aoife's accent, sounding more like "ore" than ire.

The Irishwoman looked at her and smiled. "Well, don't you look like the cat that ate the canary."

"I was just thinking," she said, emotion welling in her throat. "I've missed you. I'm glad I'm here."

The woman's eyes misted. "I am, too."

A movement in the doorway startled Eliza and her heart lurched at the sight before her.

Coyote's gaze met hers and held. "I thought I'd come by and see if Ezra has shown up yet." A corner of his mouth lifted in a grin.

Eliza laughed. "I have a feeling we won't be seeing him any time soon."

"That was quite the dressing down you gave Una." He moved into the kitchen. "Some of us have wanted to do that for years."

She shook her head. Those impulsive words now seemed reckless. "I shouldn't have been so rude."

"You were well within your rights." His silken smooth voice washed over her, causing her pulse to race wildly.

He glanced at Aoife as though just noticing her.

"Evenin', Doc." She finished drying a bowl and set it aside. "I just remembered, I need to fetch somethin' upstairs." Without another word she scurried toward the back staircase.

Coyote folded his arms. "Well, that was subtle."

Nervous flutters began in Eliza's stomach. She picked up the damp towel Aoife had left on the sink and folded it. "Are you here to check on Mother?"

"Yes." He stepped closer again. "And no. I came to see if putting small-minded old biddies in their place was a random occurrence, or if you could be called upon from time to time. You know, when the situation warrants."

She smoothed the towel over the back of one of the

chairs, well aware she was fidgeting. "I shouldn't have said what I did."

He moved closer until he stood only inches from her. "You were protecting Ruby and the boy."

"Well, I shouldn't have involved Ezra." It was getting harder and harder to find her voice.

"I think we both know he had it coming. So did Una for that matter." He chuckled. "I've never known her to stop talking unless her mouth was full."

She leaned back against the sink. Her insides had gone jittery and she could think of nothing but her wish that they would kiss again before she left. "Una seems…like a…"

She startled when his fingers brushed her chin, lifting it.

"What is it about you, Eliza Jane O'Hanlan?"

She gazed into eyes as green as a summer morning and lost all ability to speak or think. "How do you mean?"

"I can't be in the same room with you and not want to kiss you." He bent his heads toward hers, hesitating as if giving her time to think.

Her stomach dropped to her toes. "I… well…"

The warmth of his breath fanned her lips a split second before his mouth closed over hers.

Tingles rushed through her, spreading from her arms to her toes and back again. He coaxed her lips apart and she obliged, startled with the warmth of his tongue invading her mouth. It wasn't at all unpleasant, in fact, it was intoxicating.

She placed her hand on his arm, entranced to find it so hard and strong. Her other arm reached up to twine behind his neck. Silken strands brushed her skin and she tangled her fingers in them.

She lost all sense of time, willingly drowning in the sensations washing over her like a tidal wave. She wanted to stay in the moment forever.

He pulled away. "Tell me you aren't getting on that train the day after tomorrow."

She opened her eyes. Would she? A day or so back it was all she could think about. But lately, she hadn't thought of it at all. "I don't know."

His lips met hers again, and then he tore away and took a step back. "I'd better stop before I forget I'm a gentleman."

She bit her lip, wondering what might happen if he did. The space before her felt empty somehow, colder now that he had moved away. Her stomach was tangled in knots, and an odd ache had begun in her lower region.

"Have dinner with me tomorrow night, Eliza," he whispered.

"I'd like that."

Loud piano music began and Adelaide's banter could be heard from the other room.

He frowned. "What's she doing down here?"

Eliza explained that Abraham had been bringing Addie downstairs for a couple of hours each day. "It seems to have lifted her spirits considerably."

He frowned. "It's been a few weeks since she broke that ankle, but she still has to be careful not to overdo it. As long as she keeps that foot propped up, it's all right. But keep an eye on her."

She smiled, amused at how quickly he moved from seduction to physician.

The inside door to the kitchen opened and Emerald

stepped in. "There you are, Doc. Did you bring the medicine?"

He reached for his bag.

Eliza turned away. For a moment she'd forgotten how much she hated the deception involved in running this business. Worse, she'd allowed herself to nearly forget his role in it. "Is it really necessary?"

Emerald's jaw dropped. "Come again?"

"The...medicine, or whatever it is. Do we have to do this?"

"I think that's up to your mother, not us," Coyote reasoned.

"Well what would happen if you couldn't get the medicine? What would they do if it just wasn't available?" She asked, frustrated at the deception, even in at a house of ill repute.

"It happens sometimes," Emerald explained. "And when it does, we do what we gotta. But..." Her gaze moved between the two of them.

"It's okay, Em," Coyote said, handing the bottle to her. "Just make sure Addie knows it's here."

Frustration nagged at Eliza. How could she have allowed herself to be charmed into complacency? Both by him and by the town. After Emerald had gone, she turned to Coyote. "Why?"

He folded his arms. "It's how your mother chooses to run things. It's not up to us to change it."

"But you're a doctor; you took an oath." Her voice rose for effect. "How can you go along with this?"

"I have my reasons." He reached for his bag and snapped it shut. "And what's the alternative, Eliza? Have the girls go back to whoring?"

"It's a whorehouse," she said. "Isn't that what's

81

supposed to happen?"

He shook his head. "That's not up to me."

"And what if one of the men finds out what's truly going on? What then?" She threw her hands up in frustration. "We'll have a real mess on our hands then, won't we?"

"Eliza—"

She folded her arms and turned away. "I don't want to discuss it any further."

"Why don't we talk about this more tomorrow night?" he murmured, stepping closer.

She closed her eyes and pressed her fingertips to her forehead. She wanted that. She truly did. But to what end? If anything, this was a reminder that she didn't belong here, even if his kisses made her yearn to stay.

Behind her the door closed with a soft click.

She released a frustrated breath and glanced up to see Aoife at the top of the stairs. "You can't blame poor Sam for this. He's caught between the devil and the deep blue sea."

Eliza sagged into a chair as Aoife came the rest of the way down the stairs. "I don't see how."

"That's precisely why you need to talk to Adelaide."

****

"No!" Adelaide folded her arms and turned to look at the bright pink bedroom wall. The house had closed for the night and Eliza had broached her concerns.

"Mother." She quickly closed the door, worried the girls would overhear.

"I won't hear of it, 'Liza Jane. You got some nerve comin' in here tellin' me how to run *my business*." She gestured to herself with a finger, emphasizing the last two words.

"I'm simply asking if you've thought this through." She forced herself to sound calm, even though she felt anything but. "Have you ever considered what could happen if your secret got out?"

Arms folded, gaze fixed on the wall, Adelaide didn't look at her. "You think it's never crossed my mind?"

Eliza paced across the room. "There's the morality issue of hiring women out for…"

"Sex," Adelaide spat. "Don't be so afraid to say the word."

"Sex," Eliza repeated. "And then there is the morality of selling something you are not providing." She folded her arms and crossed the room once more. "Not to mention drugging men against their will, involving someone else in the deception…"

"Coyote's a big boy."

"Yes, but he also has the trust of this town." She reached the end of the room and turned.

Adelaide flicked an angry glance her way. "Why are you bringing this up now? You've been here how many days, watchin' how we do things, learnin' our ways. You knew about that elixir for days now."

"Because I've come to…" The stress left her body in a huff and she sank onto the foot of the bed. "Because I've come to care. About the girls, about you. About…him."

Adelaide turned, her face solemn. "You realize who you're lecturin' about morality, don't you?"

Eliza rested her cheek against the dark mahogany post. "I do."

"Everything you got to say I been sayin' to myself a long, long time," her mother said softly.

She heaved a sigh. "I suppose you have."

"You can't just waltz in here from New York with your uppity Aunt Cornelia ways and start tellin' me how to do somethin' I know more about than you ever will," Adelaide huffed.

"You never gave me the chance." Tears flooded her lashes and she closed her eyes, letting them slip past.

"What's that?"

"To learn about your business. About you. Not any of it. You just decided I didn't belong here." She swiped the moisture from one cheek. "You made the people here your family over your own child."

"Oh, honey."

From the corner of her eye, she saw Adelaide's arms come out, reaching for her. And ignored the gesture.

"I understand not wanting to raise a young child in this environment, I truly do. But at some point, I had the right to know. To decide for myself if I wanted to be a part of your life."

"I wanted to," Adelaide insisted. "It just never felt like the right time."

"I'm twenty-eight, Mother." A bitter laugh escaped her. "Exactly when was it going to be the right time?"

"Never, I suppose. Maybe I didn't want you to know what I've become. What I am. It was better when I was a mystery to you."

Eliza angled a glance her way. "You mean better for you."

"I know I did wrong," she sobbed. "I was only

thinkin' about myself."

"Don't do that."

"What?"

"Fall on your sword like that, as if that makes everything better." Eliza didn't release her grip on the bed post, staring out the window at the dark night sky rather than meeting her mother's gaze.

"I don't know what else to do besides admit I was wrong," Adelaide moaned. "I can't give us back all the time we lost. I did what I thought was best for you. Maybe at some point it became what was best for me."

Eliza sighed again. "That doesn't solve our current dilemma."

Adelaide shrugged. "I can't ask those girls to go back to whorin'. Some of 'em been ill-treated and battered their whole lives. This is the safest they've ever felt."

A soft chuckle escaped Eliza as she absorbed those words, reminding her of her arrival here. "So you really do run a home for wayward girls."

"In a manner of speaking, I suppose I do." Adelaide said softly. "I'd have to change everything if I took away that elixir now. I'd lose half my customers."

"You may lose all of them one day if you are ever found out." Eliza kept her gaze fixed on the window. "Not to mention what it would do to Coyote's reputation."

"Eliza, I know you've been sheltered from the real world. I guess that was my aim all along, savin' you from ugly truths. But I think because of that you tend to see life two ways; things is either right or they's wrong." Adelaide shook her head. "It ain't like that out here in the west, people do what they have to in order to survive. And whorin' is part of it."

"I suppose you and I will simply have to disagree on things, then." Defeated and exhausted from arguing, Eliza stood. "I won't argue with you about this any further. I'll pack my things and move to the hotel. I think I should go back to New York on Sunday, as planned. I'll wire Aunt Cornelia to expect me next week."

A sob from behind nearly turned her around.

At the doorway she paused. "I'm glad we finally got to know each other, even if it was too late."

Chapter Eleven

The town was abuzz with the news that Eliza Jane O'Hanlan had insulted Una Barlow in Wylder's Mercantile the day before. And that she had moved out of Miss Addie's place and into the hotel.

Coyote strode through the lobby of the Vincent House Hotel, intent on finding Eliza and learning the truth. The desk clerk sent a bellhop up to let her know she had a caller, and he paced, restlessly, while waiting for her to appear.

The young man came back, looking a bit sheepish. "She ain't comin'."

"Fine. I'll find her myself." Coyote turned and strode toward the grand staircase. He'd pound on every door if he had to.

"I don't think that's allowed, Doc," the young man called after him.

He'd no more than reached the upstairs hall when he spotted her, coming toward the stairs. She saw him and immediately turned to head the other direction.

"Oh, no you don't." He grabbed hold of her arm, halting her movements. "What in the devil is going on?"

She wrenched her arm away. "With what?"

"Your mother is in a state and the entire town is talking about you," he whispered sternly, aware of the people milling about the hallway around them.

She lifted her chin in that defiant way he'd come to find infuriating—and adorable. "Then let them talk. I simply thought it was a bit crowded at the—Mother's place and it would be best if I stayed here until I leave on Sunday."

He folded his arms. "You're supposed to be here to take care of your mother, not to break her heart."

Both fists balled at her sides and color filled her cheeks. "And you brought me here under false pretenses."

He gritted his teeth. "I wrote you because your mother is injured and needs help. That's the truth."

Tears shimmered in her eyes and she swiped at them. "She doesn't want my help; she's made that clear."

"Maybe because you aren't really trying to help. She needs someone to run her business while she is off her feet, not destroy it." He shook his head. Damn it, he didn't know whether to kiss her or strangle her. Right now he wanted to do both.

"But she's—"

By now people had opened their doors to peek out into the hallway.

"Which room is yours?" he asked.

"What?"

"You need to hear it and if Miss Addie isn't going to tell you, I will." He took hold of her elbow again, steering her down the hall. He stopped at an open doorway and recognized her bags piled in a corner of the room. He pushed her inside and closed the door behind them.

She whirled, eyes wide. "Don't you dare try to accost me."

He put his hands to his hips. "I'll ignore the insult for now. You weren't worried about me *accosting* you yesterday."

She glared at him with those soft blue eyes. "That was… yesterday. And you weren't angry with me then."

"I'm not angry with you now, just frustrated."

She gestured toward the door. "You really should leave the door open, it's not proper."

"I'm a doctor, you could be in need of medical care."

She shook her head.

"We're both adults, Eliza. We can be behind closed doors and if the town finds it scandalous, I know who to call on to put them in their place." He grinned, but the gentle teasing didn't seem to relax her.

She looked away, then back at him. "Me?" She pressed a hand to her cheeks. "I've never been like that. It's this town, I don't know what it's done to me."

"Opened your eyes to a different world maybe? One where catering to the whims of an old spinster isn't your daily routine?"

She glanced down. "I suppose so. Now what was it you needed to tell me so desperately that you are compromising my reputation and yours as well?"

"Eliza Jane O'Hanlan, when I choose to compromise you, you'll damn well know it."

"Then it better be soon because I'm leaving in two days." Two bright red splotches appeared on her cheeks. "Now I believe you had something to say."

"Every single one of those girls had a bad start in life. They were all working as prostitutes when they found their way to Wylder. Miss Adelaide took them in and cleaned them up." He put a hand to his hips, watching her for any sign of reaction. "She poured a lot of love on those girls. Love, I'm guessing, she wanted to give to her own daughter but couldn't."

Tears streamed down her cheeks.

"I know to outsiders our ways don't make sense. But they do to us here in Wylder and that's all that matters." He shook his head. Her tears might be the death of him.

She swiped at her cheeks and sniffled. "That still doesn't explain why you go along with it."

"Your mother lost one of her girls. In the early days after Willowby had just died and she was trying to get on her feet again." He sucked in a deep breath. "A soldier got a little too rough, she fought back, and he beat her. Viciously."

"Let me guess. Crystal?"

He ignored the anger and the grief that washed over him at that name. "I think that's what they called her, yes."

"I'm sorry. I know how hard you must have tried to save her."

"I wasn't here then. It was ol' doc Hanson, the sheriff's father. I got here just after she died."

"And that's when the drugging began?"

"Shortly afterward. I started out as Doc Hanson's partner until he retired. But the girls were getting hurt on a regular basis. Adelaide came to me, wanting to know what she could do to calm the men. Then Abraham came into town, a freeman looking for work. Your mother took one look at the size of him and offered him a job as her bouncer. That helped a lot, too." He pulled in a calming breath. "It all came together bit by bit."

"I've tried to talk to her but it just doesn't work." She pulled in a shaky breath. "I just keep thinking…these are the people she chose to love instead of me." She bit her lip. "I know it's childish but I can't help feeling a bit of jealousy that she cares so much for them and I'm…" she sniffed and shook her head. "When I try to talk to her, she changes the subject or we argue. We still don't know each other and maybe we never will."

He sat down on the bed beside her, placing his hand on hers. "Stop trying to change her. Just try to understand her."

She nodded. "I suppose you're right."

"And maybe, while you're at it, forgive her for not being the mother you wanted her to be." He kept his tone gentle, hoping she would listen to reason. He didn't want her to go, and her mother needed her. But the choice to stay had to come from Eliza, not from him.

Her breath hitched but before she could speak, he slipped a finger beneath her chin and bent to kiss her. Her lips softened beneath his, and he couldn't contain a moan of satisfaction. The first time he'd kissed her had been like kissing a brick wall, but apparently, she'd learned a thing or two yesterday.

Her tongue came out to meet his and he pulled her closer, pressing her tight against him. The soft, sweet smell of her teased his nostrils. The memory of how she'd looked with her hair hanging loose about her waist taunted him, and he grew hard at the memory.

Her arms came around his neck. The feel of her soft breasts crushed against him inflamed him further.

He tangled one hand in her hair, seeking the pins that held in in place.

She pulled back a bit. "What are you doing?"

He pulled one pin, and then another, watching as the reddish gold curls tumbled past her shoulders. "Compromising you."

A slight smile turned up the corners of her lips. "I see."

"You did say to make it soon." He leaned in closer, his lips hovering over hers.

She reached up to remove the remaining pins from her hair, shaking her head so that her hair fell loose. "Then I guess we'd better get to it."

He leaned her back on the bed, stretching out alongside her. "I'm not a man to take such things lightly, Eliza. If we make love, I'm not taking you to catch that train."

"And I'm not accustomed to taking orders from anyone except an old spinster woman." She pressed her lips to his, eager, which surprised him. Maybe he wasn't the only one conflicted about her leaving on Sunday.

He fumbled behind her for the buttons along the back of her dress. It had been so long since he'd been with a woman, he wasn't sure he remembered how to undress one. He didn't take his pleasure at Miss Addie's; it would be awkward to do so with women who were also his patients. He preferred to head outside of Wylder for such liaisons, but those were few and far between. The town couldn't seem to spare its doctor for long, at least not since he'd been here.

At last he'd freed the bodice and tugged it from her shoulders.

Creamy white skin and the swells of her breasts met his gaze. He ran a hand over her pale skin, amazed at the contrast, his hand, darkened from too much time outdoors, and her, as pale as fresh cream.

She trembled and he gathered her closer.

"Sam," she whispered. "I've never…"

He nodded. "I know."

He kissed her again, coaxing a response, letting them both grow acquainted to the feel and taste of one another.

He slid his hand between them, filling his palm with the softness of one breast.

Her startled gasp turned to a moan when he found the tender nipple, swollen and in need of his touch. He teased it with his thumb, stroking it until she pulled her mouth from his. Her gaze met his, her eyes heated to a darker hue of blue.

He tugged her chemise down far enough to free her breasts. He bent his head, swirling his tongue over the tender pink bud. She slid her fingers into his hair, arching toward him, crying out.

A knock came at the door.

He pulled back, his gaze meeting hers. "Were you expecting someone?"

"No one knows I'm here except you and my mother."

Another knock. "Eliza Jane O'Hanlan," came Aoife's thick brogue. "I know you're in there, child."

"Well I guess you're truly good and compromised now." He dropped a kiss to her nose and helped her up, hurriedly buttoning her dress.

"Samuel Sullivan, I know you're in there, too." This was said in a hushed whisper, as though she didn't want anyone to overhear.

He reached the door in the same second as Eliza.

Aoife stood there, dressed in her Sunday best, complete with a flowered hat pinned in her gray curls. Her startled gaze moved between the two of them, Eliza with her hair in disarray, lips swollen from kissing. And him with his shirt hastily tucked into his trousers. She stepped inside and closed the door. "Well, I can certainly see what's going on here."

"Eef, I can explain."

"Don't be ridiculous, there's nothing here to explain. Mother Nature knows what she's doing and you two have been pulling toward one another for days." She picked up his hat from where he'd set in on a chair and held it toward him. "But just the same, Samuel, You've got no business in here trifling with this girl unless you intend to marry her."

The suggestion hit him like a rock. Marry Eliza? He'd never thought of marrying again, had never met a woman who could tolerate him being available to the entire town at all hours. But she certainly was independent.

Aoife swatted him with his hat.

"Ow," he jerked back.

"Don't stand there gaping like a cod fish. Get out of this room before I send for Father O'Rorke."

He stumbled toward the door, mind spinning with what Aoife had suggested. Marry Eliza. Nothing had ever made more sense. "We're still having dinner tonight.'" He didn't phrase it as a question, didn't want to give her room to change her mind.

"I don't think—"

"She'll be havin' dinner all right," Aoife said

moving toward Eliza with a shake of her head. "And I'll be comin' along to chaperone."

****

The restaurant at the Vincent House hotel bustled with activity as Eliza and Aoife walked in. A few people turned to look at her and conversation buzzed as she walked past. Her cheeks burned. Aoife had been right about Una Barlow being a gossip.

Coyote rose as they approached his table. His hair was smoothed back and his beard trimmed. She met his gaze and a flush came over her at the memory of their earlier encounter. Her body heated all over again.

His gaze held hers a few lingering seconds, as though trying to gauge her feelings, before he turned to greet Aoife and pull out her chair.

The Irishwoman took a seat, eyes sparkling with excitement. From the way she looked around and took everything in, Eliza had the feeling her friend had never eaten in a restaurant before.

A waitress came by and greeted them warmly and read off a list of menu items.

Eliza chose the fresh river trout while Aoife and Coyote both chose beefsteak.

The waitress filled their coffee cups, placed a pot of tea on the table for Aoife and moved on.

Aoife adjusted her napkin on her lap. "Well, now that we know the two of you are physically attracted to one another…"

Eliza moaned. "Auntie Eefee—"

"It's human nature," she insisted. "But have you taken time to get to know one another?"

Eliza glanced at Coyote across the table, imploring him to change the subject. Quickly.

"For example, Sam, does the girl know you were married before?"

His brows shot up. "Well, no, I—"

"Yes." Eliza straightened in her chair. "Mother mentioned you were a widower."

"I see."

"Sam?" Aoife glanced at him and tipped her head toward Eliza. "Anything to add to that?"

"I uh…" he cleared his throat. "We were only married a few days before I left. She died in childbirth while I was away."

"Away?" Eliza asked, leaning back as the waitress set a plate before her. Another server came by and set a plate before both Aoife and Coyote.

"The war," he said.

"Sam was a sharpshooter for some Virginia regiment," Aoife supplied. She eyed the steak, which took up the entire plate, with wide eyes.

"The thirtieth Battalion Virginia Sharpshooters," he said, picking up a knife and slicing into the steak. Red juice spilled onto the plate.

"Were you a doctor then? During the war, I mean?" Eliza took a small forkful of the trout and set it on Aoife's plate for her to try. Aoife, in turn, set a slice of steak on Eliza's plate.

"No," he said. "My time in the war was what made me want to be a doctor. I watched too many of my fellow soldiers die, there was nothing I could do to help them. I didn't like that feeling." He cleared his throat. "Toward the end, I helped the field docs where I could, to make sure it was what I really wanted to do." He reached for his water and glanced up at Eliza. "How about you?"

"I...read to my aunt and tend to her meals." Her cheeks burned as she spoke. He'd lived so much and she...not at all.

"And with Cornelia Appleby that's no easy thing, I'm sure," Aoife said.

Eliza managed a wan smile. Surely, he would find her lacking, would want a much more exciting woman rather than a spinster who spent her time wishing for life to happen.

"No other family, then?" he asked.

"Not that I'm aware of. I...don't know my father's side at all." She took another forkful of trout. "Do you...have family in the area?"

"My parents and a sister are gone. I have one sister left but I haven't seen her in a long time. She, uhh...travels a lot."

Eliza noticed the way he hedged. "I see. So if you are originally from Virginia, how did you find your way to Wylder?"

"Oh, looky here," Aoife piped up. "Here comes the dessert tray."

A server came toward them carrying a tray laden with all sorts of treats. The hotel was noted for its wild blackberry pie with fresh cream.

Eliza did her best to keep the rest of the conversation light, no more hard questions. But even as the server came to clear away their dishes she wondered at the stricken look on Coyote's face when she'd asked how he'd come to Wylder.

Chapter Twelve

Early the next morning, Eliza walked the short distance from the hotel to meet Ruby and Mary McCleary behind Lowery's Dress Shoppe.

The newly widowed woman was dressed all in black, her russet curls pulled back in a severe knot at the nape of her neck. It seemed criminal for her to have to go to work only days after putting her husband in the ground.

"How are you doing, Mary?" she greeted.

"Fine." She nodded. "I'm just fine."

"Mornin', ladies." Earl Hanson, out making his morning rounds, greeted them with a tip of his hat, eyeing them with speculation.

Mary looked as if she might faint.

"Mrs. McCleary," the sheriff pinned her with a serious gaze. "I wanted to extend my condolences on the loss of your husband. He was a…fine man."

She didn't look up at him, merely fiddled with her wedding ring. "Th—thank you, Sheriff."

"Are the boys holding up all right?" he asked.

She nodded. "Yes, fine."

Eliza glanced at Ruby.

"They're doin' real good, Sheriff Hanson. Mister Russ Holt got the two older ones, Seamus and Peter, there at the ranch today, helpin' out with the horses. And the two younger ones, Danny and Mal, are spendin' some time with Doc Sullivan."

Eliza was surprised at this news.

"Well, now, I'm sure the boys will enjoy that." He tipped his hat again. "I'd best be on m'way. Mary, you take care now."

"Sheriff," Ruby spoke up. "Miss Aoife just cooked a fresh batch of her sugar cookies this morning. You should stop on by and see if you can charm a few out of her."

His ears reddened. "You tell her I'll be by."

He strolled away and Mary put a hand to her heart. "I thought sure he was about to arrest me."

Ruby put a hand to the woman's arm. "No, Mary. I told you. Coyote took care of it. Let's go find Miss Fabray now."

"How did he take care of it?" Eliza asked as they made their way down the alley.

Ruby shrugged. "I dunno, but around here when the doc says he's gonna take care of somethin', he just does."

As they approached the back of the dress shop, they noticed a small, dark-haired man bent over a washboard, scrubbing frantically. Around him, three washpots bubbled away on fires. Even at this early hour, the lines were full of clean, wet clothing hung to dry.

As they approached, he removed his floppy hat. Dark hair spilled to her shoulders. Amber eyes flashed recognition and Eliza realized this was not a man at all but a young woman. A very pretty woman dressed in men's clothing.

"Mornin', Ruby," she greeted. "You got some wash for me?" She eyed Eliza somewhat warily.

"Ma'am?"

"This here's Miz Eliza O'Hanlan," Ruby said by way of introduction. "Miss Addie's daughter. And this here is Missus McCleary. Did Miz Lowery tell you she was comin'?"

The girl wiped a hand over her brow. "She did."

Eliza glanced about at the piles of laundry in various stages. "It looks as though Mary has come at the right time. This is a lot of laundry for one person."

Beside her, Mary rolled up the sleeves of her black dress. "Let me help."

"I think you're just s'posed to be ironing," the girl said.

She moved in beside the girl and took up a scrubbing board. "I can help with laundry, too, I don't mind."

Eliza exchanged glances with Ruby; apparently the two women would get on just fine.

They strolled in silence toward the corner, watching the small town wake from its slumber. Businesses were just beginning to open, women holding the hands of young children and carrying baskets hurried toward the mercantile. Finn Wylder paused in propping open the door to wave toward them.

At the corner, Eliza turned to Ruby. "I guess this is goodbye then."

The girl's brown eyes welled with emotion. "Now, Miss Eliza, you ain't really gettin' on that train on Sunday, are ya?"

It was Eliza's turn to feel emotion. "I think it's for the best."

"Your mama's just heartbroke at the thought of you two leavin' things like this. And so are us girls,"

Ruby said.

"I just don't think we'll ever agree on...certain things."

Ruby glanced around, as though afraid of being overheard. "I know what you two argued about, we all do."

Eliza's cheeks flamed. "I'm sorry. I've come to realize that it's none of my business."

The girl put her hand on Eliza's arm. "No, that's exactly what it is. When Miss Addie is gone someday, it will be yours. 'Til then you and your mama just gotta learn to trust each other."

"I don't see how that's possible."

"Miss Eliza, I ain't never seen your mama so happy as she's been these last few days, havin' you here." She lifted her brows. "And I don't think Doc Sullivan has ever been so attentive to a patient before."

"My mother is certainly a force to be reckoned with."

Ruby laughed. "That Miss Adelaide is, but I meant he's been comin' around for another reason. You."

Eliza blanched and looked down at the boardwalk beneath her feet. Despite all that had happened with Coyote and the wonderful new feelings he had inspired, her life was in New York. Everything that had happened since she'd arrived in Wylder only convinced her she didn't belong here. "I'm sure that's not the case."

"You ain't never gonna find out if you leave."

****

Eliza spent much of the morning alone in her hotel room, preparing for the next day's departure. She wrote letters to her mother and to Aoife and each of the girls, apologizing for her hasty departure.

The thought of returning to New York weighed heavily on her. How could she go back to taking care of Aunt Cornelia when she'd had such a wonderful taste of freedom here in Wylder? She'd miss Mother and Aoife terribly and even the girls themselves. And poor Mary McCleary, she hoped the woman embraced her new start in life and found the happiness she deserved.

The most difficult letter to write was for Coyote. In fact, she couldn't bring herself to write that one. A part of her wanted to stay and explore the fascinating sensations between them. But she couldn't, not with the nagging worry about him providing the medicine to drug Mother's clients. And his willing participation in the scheme.

Instead she gathered up her things and set out once again, walking down Wylder Street. The morning sun had given way to afternoon heat and she enjoyed a leisurely stroll as she made her way down the street. She paused to listen at the outdoor theatre as someone in costume stood on the stage and recited lines to an empty audience. She recognized it as the final scene from Macbeth and wondered when the play would begin.

Who would have thought to find Shakespeare here in Wylder? She was sorry she would have to miss it. She came to corner of Sidewinder Lane, but rather than cross directly to the doctor's office, she chose to keep walking toward the mercantile.

As she passed the dress shop, she waved through the window to Laurel Adams. The dark-haired seamstress was taking Una Barlow's measurements. The girl smiled, earning Eliza a glare from Mildred

Lowery for disturbing her employee. And right alongside Ms. Fabray, Mary was ironing on the porch. Mary didn't have much to say but Leona didn't seem to mind, she chattered away like a magpie, pausing to wave hello as Eliza passed by.

Finn Wylder stood outside the mercantile, sweeping the step. Two elderly gentlemen sat on opposite sides of a barrel, checkboard between them. They nodded a greeting then returned to their game. "Morning, Miss O'Hanlan," he greeted warmly. "What can I do for you today?"

She smiled at him. "Mister Wylder, I fear I owe you an apology for my behavior the other night."

He stopped sweeping and regarded her with warm brown eyes filled with understanding. "Whatever for?"

"What I said to...to Mrs. Barlow. I had no cause to be so rude with a guest in your store."

"I'd say you had plenty of cause," he said. "You called her exactly what she is—judgmental and sanctimonious."

"She's an old cow." This from one of the men at the checkerboard.

"Always was a fat little thing," the other man said. "Even as a youngster she was into everybody's business but her own."

"Dad," Finn warned. "Let's be nice."

"That *was* nice, I could have said worse." Bushy white brows wiggled with mischief. "In my day we called her Heels Up Una."

Eliza smiled at the older gentleman's innocent expression. He winked at her and returned to his game. "Well, I should have held my tongue and not caused a scene."

"I'd beg to differ, she's the one who should hold her tongue." Finn leaned on the broom handle. "I'm sorry to hear you'll be leaving us soon."

She was surprised at this. Apparently, news traveled fast in a small town like Wylder. "It's time I got back to New York to continue caring for my aunt. This has been a most pleasant diversion, but I'm afraid I'm not cut out for life in the west." She'd made up her mind, so why were these simple goodbyes so difficult?

"Well, we'll certainly be sorry to see you go."

"Yep," echoed the senior Mr. Wylder. "We like havin' the pretty ones around. We got enough old hags like Una."

"Amen to that," said his companion with an impish grin.

Eliza turned to go, hurrying across the road toward the doctor's office.

As she passed the hotel, she noted the doctor's buggy in the alleyway and Harley tied in the shade nearby. Her pulse raced and her breath felt short at the thought of seeing him again, but she steadied herself.

She stepped inside his office. The room was dark and a bit stuffy in the mid-day heat. A shelf along one wall was cluttered with various bottles and powders as well as a mortar and pestle. A chair in front of it held the doctor's bag, left wide open.

On the other wall was a desk with a bookshelf over it. This shelf, too, was cluttered with various books and papers. An odd-looking device sat atop the desk and on closer inspection she recognized it a printing device called a typewriter. She'd heard of such things, but most people couldn't afford them and she'd never seen one before.

One small window was blocked by a collection of books and more papers and she had to resist the urge to move them aside to let in some light. The flour sack curtain that covered the window looked old and dusty enough to have been placed there by the original doctor.

"Can't turn my back on you two for a minute, can I?"

Muffled voices came from a room off of this one. A peek inside the doorway showed Coyote with the youngest McCleary boy seated on a table. The young boy's head was tipped back and Coyote held a large pair of tweezers to his nostrils.

She paused in the doorway, enjoying the gentle tone as he spoke to the little boy.

"Haven't we talked about this before, Mal? You simply don't go around sticking things up your nose. Just because it's small enough to fit up there doesn't mean it needs to go in."

Malachy pointed toward his brother, who stood nearby, watching the procedure with great interest. "That was him."

"It *was* you wasn't it, Danny? I guess this is a McCleary family tradition." Coyote turned to look over his shoulder. His brows raised when he caught sight of her in the doorway. "This is an unexpected surprise. Unless of course you're here for a medical reason?"

"No," she shook her head and came farther into the room. "Anything I can do to help?"

"Yes, find me some twine to tie this young man's fingers together so he'll stop putting marbles up his nose."

The boy giggled, then pulled a face as Coyote eased his head back again.

Eliza moved in closer. "You know my friend, Ruby, don't you?"

Malachy nodded.

"She told me what a big brave boy you are and what a help you've been to your mama." Noting his wiggly legs, she moved closer, settling a hand on his knee.

"I'm four," he said, holding up the fingers of one hand to show her.

"My goodness, you're big for four, are you sure you aren't older?" She placed a hand on his other knee while talking, keeping him still while Coyote continued to probe with the tweezers. She continued to talk, asking him any and all questions she could think of until finally, she heard the clink of something in a cup.

"There we go."

Both young Danny and Malachy leaned in to look at the mucus covered marble, pulling faces at the sight of it.

Coyote lifted him off the table. "Now that better be the last time or I'll get a rope and tie your arms down to your sides until you're twelve."

"Yeah, then how would you pick your nose?" the older brother chided.

The younger boy giggled, even as one finger went up to probe his nose.

Coyote reached into his pocket and pulled out a coin. "Why don't you two head over to the mercantile for some candy. I need to talk to Miss O'Hanlan."

Danny grabbed the coin eagerly and the two scampered off. "And stay away from your mother at the dress shop or Mrs. Lowery will tan both your hides," he called after them.

He turned to face her, hands on his hips. "You think I should have told him to keep the candy out of his nose?"

She laughed.

He gestured for her to head out into the other room. "Thank you, by the way, for holding him down. I was getting kicked pretty good every time I tried to grab that marble."

She stepped into the room, once again struck by how dark and uninviting it felt, overcome with the urge to tidy up. He stood, rested one hip against the desk, facing her.

"So you're not here for a medical reason. I'm guessing it's to say goodbye."

"I…how did you know?"

"Word travels fast around here. Everyone knows you moved to the hotel the other day. And you were seen in the rail office early this morning." He shrugged. "It's not hard to guess why."

Her cheeks began to feel warm. "I guess the whole town knows my business."

One corner of his mouth lifted in a grin. "Everyone here knows everyone's business." He shifted, studying her with those intense green eyes. "So you and your mother couldn't resolve your differences?"

"I didn't try," she admitted. "We left things as they were and…I guess I don't see the point in continuing to argue about it." Unable to bear the scrutiny, she moved toward the window, brushing the dust off the books on the ledge. "I realize it puts her at a disadvantage, but I think with Abraham helping her to get up and down the stairs, she is better able to—" She felt the heat of him behind her.

"It certainly puts us at a disadvantage, doesn't it?"

"I've told you from the beginning that I wouldn't be staying." She turned, he was so close her nose nearly brushed his chest. Warmth bathed her insides at the memory of his hands on her body the other day. What would have happened if Aoife hadn't come by? "I really should go, if the town is so inquisitive about the movements of others, they will surely notice I'm in here alone with you."

"For all they know I'm examining a patient." He closed the distance between them, his hand sliding to her hips. "Maybe I should start."

She placed a hand to his chest but the attempt to halt him turned to a caress as his lips met hers.

The ground beneath her feet tilted and she leaned against him.

"Marry me, Eliza," he whispered against her lips.

"You don't know anything about me, how can you possibly propose?"

His hands came up to her face. "You go out of your way to help a woman find work after losing her husband. You fight to defend a kind-hearted girl and a little boy when they're being insulted by a mean old pea hen. You know how to distract a child while his nose is being probed. What more do I need to know?"

She shook her head. "That's not me at all. I can't even stand up to an old spinster woman who yells at me because her tea is too cold or too hot or has too much sugar or not enough." Tears spilled past her lashes. "It's this town, it's done something to me."

"It does that to all of us." He dropped a kiss to her nose, but still didn't move away. "So why would you want to go back to that?"

"Because I don't belong here."

"So better to be an unpaid servant to a bully?"

"It's preferable to staying here and living in my mother's shadow. Besides, Aunt Cornelia needs me, and—"

"Eliza," he sighed. "You're running scared."

Maybe she was. But she'd made up her mind. "I should go."

"Then at least kiss me goodbye."

She'd never wanted anything so much in her life. She moved closer, leaned in until his lips brushed hers. He deepened the kiss, thrusting his tongue into her mouth, and she sighed, leaning against him. How would she ever live out the rest of her days knowing what it was to be kissed by him and never experiencing it again?

"How dare you?" An irate voice came from the doorway. "In here carrying on with this Jezebel while these two ruffians accost me?"

Eliza jumped. She turned to see none other than Una Barlow, face red with fury, her dress splattered with mud. She had young Daniel McCleary by the collar of his shirt and little Mal by the upper arm.

She shoved the two boys toward him. "Am I to understand, Doctor Sullivan, that you are in charge of these hellions today?"

As she stepped into the office a foul odor assailed Eliza's nose. "What is that?"

"Horse manure," Danny said matter-of-factly.

Young Mal proudly held up two soiled hands to show her. "We threw poop at the mean lady."

Eliza glanced at Mrs. Barlow. Oh dear, so the stain on her dress was not mud at all…

"Let's go out back and wash up," Coyote said, his tone stern.

Danny hung his head, looking guilty. "You gonna give us a whuppin' Doc?"

"If he doesn't, I will," Una insisted.

"Una, they were just being boys. I'll be sure to keep a closer eye on them." He glanced at the woman then to Eliza. "Are you coming?"

"I'll be along in a minute." Eliza waited until the boys were gone before turning to face the older woman.

"You," the woman seethed. "In here doing God knows what with that poor excuse for a doctor while those little hoodlums are out wreaking havoc." She turned toward the door. "I've got a good mind to tell my dear friend Mildred Lowery to fire Mary McCleary for the way her children behaved today."

Anger surged down Eliza's spine. "Perhaps she'd be more interested in how your late husband spent his Saturday evenings. I understand it involved spanking him and telling him what a naughty boy he was."

The woman stopped at the door to peer over her shoulder, eyes narrowed. "You wouldn't dare."

She folded her arms. "Mother keeps meticulous records. I'm sure there are more than a few entries on Ezra."

"Harlot!"

"Actually it's Eliza Jane," she said. "And before you head to the dress shop, you might want to go home and change. You smell worse than the livery."

With a huff, the woman stomped out the door. Without waiting for her to clear the front steps, Eliza turned and rushed toward the back of the house.

She pushed the back door open, afraid she'd find

the boys being "whupped" but instead found Coyote standing by while they scrubbed their hands. No one looked as if they'd had a beating. In fact, they were giggling as they told him about their escapade. He seemed to be struggling to keep a stern expression.

She lingered for a moment longer, absorbing the sound of childish laughter, and Coyote's deep chuckle as Danny mimicked Mrs. Barlow's walk and facial expressions.

Heart heavy, she turned and silently closed the door.

This would have to suffice for a goodbye.

Chapter Thirteen

One moment she was there, the next she was gone. Coyote couldn't hide his disappointment at Eliza slipping away as she did, but he understood that she would want to avoid a long goodbye.

He made Danny and Mal do chores the rest of the afternoon as punishment and refused to let them go to the mercantile to get the candy they'd never gotten around to purchasing.

Truth was, he didn't blame them for wanting to get back at Una Barlow.

Mary came by to pick up the boys a little after six when the dress shop closed. He told her about the Una incident, and assured her he had already punished the two for pelting the woman with horse manure.

She looked exhausted and instead of having her walk the four miles back home, he gave her and the boys a ride in his buggy. The trip had given him a chance to pull the older two McCleary boys aside. They'd both appeared shocked when he'd told them he knew Seamus had been the one to pull the trigger and kill Red. It wasn't hard to guess that as the oldest son he'd feel the obligation to protect his mother and younger brothers.

He'd assured the boy he'd done nothing wrong and that the sheriff wouldn't be looking into things any further. The relief on the lad's face was all he needed to know he'd done the right thing.

Maybe it wasn't his place as a doctor to get involved in the lives of his patients, but sometimes the law was a little too cut-and-dried and didn't allow for situations like Mary's.

Earl was too dedicated a lawman to let anything stand in the way of justice. Coyote was just glad he'd been able to smooth the situation over. Hopefully Mary and her boys would have a better life with Red gone.

"You playin' or daydreamin', Doc?" Russ Holt asked around a cloud of cigar smoke.

Startled from his reverie, he drew a card from the deck on the table. He'd spent the better part of the evening in the Five Star Saloon, playing poker with Russ and Caleb Holt, Earl Hanson, and the livery owner, Chet Daniels.

Russ wore a smug expression. "You should know word around town is you've been trifling with Addie's girl," he said, smoke curling past his nostrils. "She's practically my stepdaughter. Should I be worried about your intentions?"

"Nope," Coyote said, drawing another card from the deck and trying not to frown. Aces and eights were always bad luck. "She's heading back to New York tomorrow morning."

"Addie know that?" Caleb asked over his hand of cards, the kid had already won the last two hands of five-card draw.

"She does by now." Coyote picked up his glass and tossed back the contents. "The whole town is talking about it."

"That'll break her heart," Russ said, eyeing his cards. He scratched his cheek and Coyote noticed his foot jiggling beneath the table. Maybe his hand wasn't as good as his face suggested.

"Well, she's the only one who could have gotten Eliza to stay and she didn't ask," he pointed out. "They're both too stubborn for their own good." He glanced over at the sheriff. "Earl? You in?"

Earl tossed another chip on the pile. "Yeah, I'm in."

Caleb was just reaching for a card when a loud commotion came from outside.

Two men burst through the batwing doors. "Shots fired at Miss Addie's place!"

Coyote's blood ran cold. "Miss Addie's? You sure?" He jumped from his seat, not caring that the chair clattered to the floor. Beside him, Earl struggled to his feet, favoring his bad knee.

"Doc, you better come," the first man said. "I hear one of the girls is hurt bad."

Russ was already at the door. "You got your bag, Doc?"

"With my horse," he said.

"Go on ahead," Caleb called. "I'll come with the sheriff."

Nothing had ever taken as long as the ride to the brothel. Russ was right behind him but neither of them spoke. He supposed the other man was just as worried.

It probably took less than five minutes to cross Old Cheyenne Road near the post office and take the horses across the tracks. Yet it felt endless.

A crowd of men were gathered on the porch outside, all of them trying to tell him what had happened. "Step aside," Russ ordered. "Let the doc through."

114

Coyote took the stairs to the second floor two at a time, Russ close at his heels.

In the second-floor hallway, Miss Addie sat on the floor, her leg twisted at an awkward angle. A rifle sat on the floor beside her and a new hole in the roof showed a sprinkling of stars overhead. Abraham was slumped in the doorway. Beside him, Emerald held a blood-soaked cloth to his left arm.

The instant they saw him, everyone began talking at once. Adelaide burst into tears at the sight of Russ. Coyote stopped to check on her but Russ waved him on.

"I got her, Doc," he said, gathering the tiny woman into his arms. "Come on, Addie, let's get you to bed."

The fact that she only nodded and didn't crack a joke concerned Coyote a little, but there was no time to worry about it right now. He stopped and knelt down in front of Abraham. "What happened?"

Abraham nodded toward the room where Aoife and the other girls stood around a bed. "It's Amethyst. Soldier beat her up pretty bad. I tried to get in but he had the door jammed." He winced. "I knocked it down and he came at me with a knife."

"Let me see the arm."

Abraham shook his head. "I'm not hurt bad, Doc. I can wait. You jus' take care of Miss Amethyst."

Inside the room, he hurried the other women out of the way so he could examine the injured woman. Her face was battered and bruised, one eye swollen shut. Both arms and knuckles held bruises that suggested she'd fought back.

"I'm okay, Doc," she slurred. "I gave him as good as I got. Abraham okay?" The halting way she spoke and her pale color told him she had at least one broken rib. He'd know more once he got a look at her.

He nodded. "I'm sure he is, but he asked me to take care of you first."

Aoife stood near the bed, a worried expression on her face. "He caught her puttin' more drops in his drink," she explained. "By the time we heard the screams and Abraham got up here—" Her eyes welled and she dabbed at them with her apron.

Amethyst reached for the woman's hand. "I'm fine, Eef."

"I'll be the judge of that," he said, opening his bag to find his stethoscope. "Mind if I examine you?"

"Doc, you know how we girls feel about you," she said again, halting between words as though speaking was painful. "Examine anything you want, no charge." She tried to laugh but moaned and touched a hand to her swollen lip.

"It's okay, luv," Aoife cooed, stroking her hair. "I'm gonna take good care of ya." She looked up the other girls standing around the bed, wide-eyed. "Go on with ya now, git!"

They hurried out of the room, practically tripping over one another.

Coyote finished his exam, wrapping her ribs with Aoife's help. He would know more once the swelling went down, but internal injuries and the possibility of a punctured lung weighed heavy on his mind. He'd have Aoife keep a close eye on her and check back daily until the girl was back on her feet. "Where's the man who did this?"

Amethyst shrugged. "Lit on outta here after he stabbed poor Abraham."

He opened his bag to put away his stethoscope and other instruments. "Do you know who it was?"

"No, but I bet he's got a few bruises of his own." She tried to smile but moaned and touched her lip again.

"You get some rest, young lady, no entertaining until I say so."

She nodded. "Sure, Doc."

He turned to Aoife, who stood by, wringing her hands in her apron, and handed her a jar from his bag. "Dover's Powders. Every six hours or if she can't sleep."

Aoife nodded, glancing over at the bed with a worried expression. "It was one of those soldiers from the fort," she said in a low voice. "Always pawin' at the girls. He was in here the other night makin' fun o' Eliza's big words."

A movement in the doorway caught his eye. Eliza whirled with a flurry of skirts, her footfalls retreating down the hall.

"Oh, Lord," Aoife said. "Let me talk to her."

When he'd finished with Amethyst, he returned to Abraham, surprised to see Emerald neatly stitching up the slash on the man's arm.

"Am I doin' all right, Doc?"

"You're doing a fine job, Em," he said, studying the tidy stitches. "Better than I could do. Where'd you learn how to do that?"

She shrugged. "My mama taught me. She was a slave, you know. She stitched up her fair share of folks got hurt. She learned from my grandmammy and I learned from her."

He stayed, watching while she worked,

unaccustomed to observing instead of doing. When she finished tying off the stitches, he handed her a knife to cut the threads.

Abraham's dark brown eyes were dull with pain, but his gaze never left Emerald's face until she finished. "Miss Amethyst all right in there?"

"She's a strong girl," Coyote assured him.

"She's a fighter, I can tell you that," the other man said with a chuckle. "Miss Addie don't let 'em keep weapons in their rooms, she's afraid of what could happen. But she didn't say nothin' about fryin' pans— Miss Amethyst keeps one under her mattress and she clocked him good."

Emerald sat back on her heels and regarded him with a raised brow. "And just how do you know what's under her mattress?"

Coyote grinned and pushed to his feet. "I think you're in trouble now, Abraham." He patted the other man on the shoulder. "I'll be by tomorrow to check on you. "He turned to Emerald. "I gave Aoife a jar of Dover's Powder, let her know if he needs it for the pain."

"I will, Doc. Thank you."

He nodded. From the way the two were eyeing one another, he had the feeling Abraham wouldn't be thinking about his arm for long.

Down the hall, the sound of hysterical tears led him to Adelaide's room. Russ sat with her on the bed, looking helpless as she sobbed into his chest.

"Addie?" Coyote asked, drawing her attention. He'd never seen the madam rattled like this.

She looked up from Russ's arms. "Oh, Coyote." She reached for him, still sobbing. "How is she?"

"All right—both of them," he assured her. "I'm a little worried about that ankle of yours, though."

She eyed him warily. "It's bad, Doc. I know I shouldn't have gotten up but I didn't think. Abraham had just brung me back upstairs, I was in my room when I heard Amethyst screamin'." Her breath hitched and she sniffled. "I grabbed my shotgun from beside the bed and tore down the hall." She gestured toward her ankle. "Somethin' snapped and I went down like a sack of flour and the gun went off." Tears began to spill. "I saw poor Abraham. For a second I thought I'd shot him."

Russ patted her hand. "Emerald's takin' care of him, he'll be fine. And I'll fix the hole in the roof, Addie, not to worry."

"Coyote, Eliza was here. I...I told her about Crystal."

His blood ran cold. That was something he had wanted to do himself. "You what?"

"How she was your sister an' all. I'm sorry, I was just so upset, it was all I could think about. 'Cause the last time this happened..." She began to sob again and Russ handed her a lacy handkerchief.

"Amethyst isn't Crystal, Addie. And the girls have all learned a thing or two since that happened."

She nodded. "I hope so."

"Where is Eliza now?"

"I don't know but you've got to talk some sense into her. Please don't let her leave tomorrow. I need to apologize and to tell her—" The blood drained from her face. "Oh Lord. My rifle." Both men turned to follow her gaze as she pointed toward the doorway. "Russ left it right there. That's where Eliza Jane was standin'—

and it's gone."

Chapter Fourteen

It wasn't safe for a woman to go strolling about town alone on a Saturday night. Drunken cowboys, ranch hands with money in their pockets and rowdy soldiers enjoying a weekend leave were among the dangers.

But none of them bothered Eliza as she stomped across the railroad tracks and down the road. In fact, they all gave her a rather wide berth. The rifle she carried may have had something to do with that.

She pulled in a deep breath to steel herself before pushing open the doors to the Five Star Saloon. Several men were present, and a hush came over the room as she stepped inside.

"Something we can help you with, honey?" asked the dark-haired man behind the bar.

"Yes. I'm looking for a soldier." A chorus of whistles met her ears and she hefted the rifle, slowly making her way into the middle of the room. "I'm not sure of his name but you can recognize him by the dimwitted expression on his face and a yellow streak down his back."

A whoop of laughter went up.

The barkeep barely paused in wiping out a glass. "What do you need him for, honey?"

She turned to face the man, swinging the rifle with her. Every man at the bar dropped to the floor. "I most certainly am not your 'honey' and I don't care for your condescending tone."

Some of the men began to slide away, taking cover under tables or behind the bar.

Except for one. He strolled out from an alcove, eyeing her suspiciously. Fresh red scratches marred his cheeks and a large purplish bruise covered one side of his face.

She lifted the rifle. "I understand you were in the Social Club this evening."

He shrugged. "Might'a been."

"I understand you hurt one of my girls."

One brow shot up. "*Your* girls?"

"Yes, mine." She adjusted the weight of the rifle. "Those girls are my family. You lay a finger on them and you answer to me."

The folly of her actions began to dawn on her. She hadn't thought things through, she had simply reacted. Exactly what she'd been doing since arriving in Wylder. Damn this town.

He set his drink on the bar and smirked. "Oh yeah? And what are you gonna do, use more big words to scold me?"

She hoped the trembling in her knees wasn't evident. "Don't move."

He strolled toward her. "Looks to me like you don't even know how to hold a rifle, much less shoot one."

The rapid clip of horse hooves came a split second before the saloon doors burst open. Heavy equine feet clomped across the wood floor and the whicker of a horse came from behind. Eliza turned. "What on earth—"

"Coyote," said the man behind the bar. "You can't—"

"There was no place to hitch my horse, Cash, and I'm in a hurry."

An arm snaked around Eliza's throat and she caught a glint of silver as a blade was held beneath her chin. "Drop your rifle, lady."

"Go to hell," she snarled.

The soldier laughed. "Think you're tough now that the doc's here to protect you, don't you?"

"Take it easy," Coyote said. "No one has to get hurt here."

The solider shifted, dragging her back a few inches. "Doc, I'm gonna need you to get down off that horse."

Coyote's brows went up. "You want to add horse theft and kidnapping to the charges you already face?"

"I don't see the sheriff here, do you?"

Eliza felt the tremor that moved through the soldier's body. The rifle weighed heavily on her arm, but she had no intention of dropping it. She kept her gaze on Coyote, noting the way one hand had gone lax at his side.

The solider pressed his arm tighter, dragging her backward another step. "I said get off the horse, dammit. And put your hands where I can see 'em."

Coyote complied. "You realize I can't dismount without using my hands."

"Just—just hurry it up." He dragged Eliza back another step. He trembled so bad she feared he might slip and cut her throat.

Coyote climbed off the horse, his gaze never leaving the solider. "All right, I'm off. Now what?"

"Just move aside—all of you." He eased back another step. "Stay out of the way while I take this little lady and leave."

As they moved back, something bumped against Eliza's hip. She glanced down and caught sight of a wooden ladder-back chair. As he dragged her with him toward the door, she trailed a hand down beside her. The moment her fingers brushed wood, she grabbed hold and pushed. The chair hit the floor with a loud clatter. The man jerked and looked behind him.

A shot rang out and the soldier dropped. It happened so fast she didn't even have time to scream. In an instant she was free and the man lay on the floor, bleeding from a shoulder wound.

Coyote strode forward to take the knife laying forgotten on the floor. "You're lucky I've had my fill of killing." He lifted the man by the shirt and socked him square in the jaw. "That's from Amethyst."

He straightened, his gaze falling on Eliza. "Give me that." He wrenched the rifle from her hands. "That's about the dumbest thing I've ever seen you do."

Words escaped her. "I…"

He walked back to his horse and motioned for Eliza to follow. "Starting tomorrow, I'm teaching you how to shoot."

"But I'm lea—"

He gave her a look that instantly silenced her. "Your mother broke that ankle again trying to get to Amethyst and Abraham. You might need to stay a little longer."

He lifted her onto the horse, then mounted behind her. "Cash, I'll be back for the soldier. And I'll pay you for any damages." With that, the horse turned and moved toward the doors.

Outside the night air wrapped around her. She paused for a few seconds to drink in the smell of the town, the peaceful quiet night and the sprinkling of stars overhead.

Coyote's arm about her waist pressed tight. "Are you all right?"

She settled back against his chest, feeling warmer and more secure than she could ever remember.

Home. He felt like home.

"Yes," she said. "But I think there is someplace I would like to go. Would you mind escorting me?"

Chapter Fifteen

The sun was already brightening the sky by the time Coyote arrived home. He had returned to the saloon to treat the soldier's wound and deliver him to the sheriff. Then he'd stopped back at the Social Club to check and re-splint Adelaide's ankle. Now he prayed for a few hours of sleep before someone else had an emergency.

He still wasn't sure why Eliza had wanted to come here, rather than the hotel, but thoughts of her kept his mind occupied while he rubbed down, fed and bedded Harley for the night. The gelding looked as bone-weary as he felt. It was one of the reasons why he chose to buy a second horse. As the town got bigger, he got busier. Having a second horse would allow this one to rest when it needed to.

If only getting a second doctor in place was as easy.

He glanced at his pocket watch as he made his way toward the door. Five a.m. He'd have to take Eliza to the hotel to gather her things and meet the train in a few hours, whether he liked it or not. He couldn't force her to stay. Life in a town like this wasn't for everyone, certainly not a city girl like her.

As he stepped inside, the smell of lemon oil and fresh morning air greeted him. "What the—"

Sunlight spilled through the newly cleaned window

on the opposite side of the room. The old curtain was gone, as were the stacks of books and papers that sat in front of it. The glass was scrubbed clean, allowing light to spill into the room.

His desk was cleared, the books neatly stacked on their shelves. The bottles and jars had been put back in their places and the thick coat of dust that had been on the bottles and shelves for as long as he could remember was gone.

But it was the sight of Eliza, her head resting on his desk, that caused his heart to swell.

He knelt down, not wanting to startle her, and brushed her cheek with his finger. Her eyes fluttered open and he was once again struck by the cornflower blue color.

"Miz O'Hanlan, it would appear someone has broken into my office and cleaned it. Would you mind chasing down the culprit or hasn't Earl deputized you yet?"

A pink flush stole over her cheeks. "I suppose the whole town is talking about my foolish venture?"

"They are."

She yawned and sat up. "You aren't angry, are you?"

"About the foolishness of you barging into a saloon and threatening a man with a weapon you don't know how to use?" He straightened.

"No. About me cleaning up in here."

"Not at all. Some of that dust was here before me, though, I didn't feel right kicking it out." He grinned, drinking in the sight of her face first thing in the morning, the way she looked just waking up.

"Did the sheriff arrest that soldier?"

"Yes, he's taking him back to the fort this morning to let the military deal with him." He cleared his throat. "I suppose you want me to take you to the train station."

She straightened in the chair. "About that. I was thinking. It really does need a woman's touch." She gestured around the room. "And maybe a good cleaning every now and then."

He folded his arms. "You're suggesting I hire a housekeeper?"

She bit her lip, looking a bit uncertain. "Actually I was hoping you'd allow me to reconsider your offer."

"Which one would that be?" His heart lurched with hope, but he couldn't resist teasing her.

She laughed and rose to her feet. "Your offer of marriage."

He opened his arms and pulled her closer. "I don't know, that was before I knew you were a gun-toting woman with a hot temper."

"As I've said, it's this town. I don't know what came over me."

"Wylder came over you. It happens to all of us."

She gazed into his eyes, her face serious. "Is Mother all right?"

He nodded. "Resting. But she wants to see you today." He sighed and studied her face. It didn't seem possible that a week ago he didn't even know her. Now he couldn't imagine life without her by his side.

"How did you accomplish that? As upset as she was, I can't imagine that she's resting."

He shrugged. "I gave her a taste of her own medicine."

She pulled back to study his face. "You what?"

He grinned. "I had Aoife bring her some tea with a good dose of the elixir in it. She'll sleep for a few hours at least. And Russ is staying with her."

"Coyote—about the elixir. I'm so sorry. It was none of my business and I had no right to—"

"You were right." He said, giving her waist a gentle squeeze. "I don't need to involve myself in that. The lady who runs the new apothecary next door knows a lot more about herbs than I ever will. I'm going to talk to her about your mother's situation and see if she can come up with something. Then I'll step out of it and leave them to it." He dropped a kiss to her nose.

"I'm glad."

"Me, too. After what happened to Kathleen—Crystal, as she was known here, I felt obligated to help Addie protect the girls. I suppose in my own way I was trying to make it up to Kathleen, for not getting here in time to save her. But it's been long enough. It's time I let it go."

"Mother told me she was your sister. I'm so sorry. What happened to her?"

"She met a man not unlike your stepfather," he sighed and leaned in, touching his forehead against hers. "Lots of promises, most of which were broken. He finally abandoned her and left her heartbroken and alone. I spent years after the war ended trying to find her, and when I did, it was too late."

"What happened to the man who beat her?"

"He's dead."

She searched his face, the question there obvious.

"It's the last man I ever killed. Those days are over." He pulled back far enough to meet her gaze. "Eliza, I don't want to talk about this anymore. In fact,

I'd prefer not to talk at all."

She glanced at his mouth, and then back up to his eyes. "What did you have in mind?"

"Well, I never did get to finish compromising you."

"That's true."

"You have no idea what finding you here waiting has done to me."

She slid her hands into the hair at the nape of his neck. "Show me."

He leaned in to take her lips, making no pretense about his intentions.

Neither did she.

Her mouth opened beneath his and she pressed against him.

He pulled away just far enough to separate their mouths. "So...you're not leaving then?"

She shook her head. "Not."

He scooped her into his arms. "There's a loft upstairs. It's not much of a bedroom but it's where I sleep when I'm here."

She wrapped her arms about his neck, holding on while he carried her up the staircase. He set her on the bed. The entire upstairs smelled of fresh air and the linens had been changed, the blanket pulled back.

"I see someone cleaned up here as well."

Her cheeks reddened. "Well, I hoped I might be invited to stay."

He set her before him, eyeing her as he unbuttoned his shirt. He shrugged it off and leaned in to kiss her again. She ran her hands over his chest, fingers tracing scars from war wounds, sliding over his shoulders and biceps.

"My turn," she whispered, reaching behind her to unfasten her shirtwaist. She untucked it from her skirt and pulled it off over her head.

He gazed on the creamy swells of her breasts rising above her chemise. Unable to help himself, he reached to trace the outline of one plump breast, sliding a finger along until he traced the outline of her nipple against the fabric.

Eliza sucked in a breath and reached to untie the ribbon that held it closed. She parted the material, easing it from her shoulders little by little. No man had ever seen her like this and she hoped he wouldn't be disappointed. She gave one last tug and cool air met her skin. Followed by the heat of his hands.

Nothing had ever felt so wonderful. No words came to mind, she was too overcome by sensation. She met his mouth eagerly, moaning as he caressed her breasts. His fingers teased her nipples and the ache that had begun deep in her core intensified with every touch. She wound her arms around his neck, sighing as his silken hair brushed the insides of her wrists.

It was as though she'd never experienced sensation before. Her body instinctively craved more, and with every touch the longing intensified.

His hands moved from her waist to cup and caress her breasts, stroking both at the same time until she thought she would go mad from pleasure.

When she could stand it no more, she unfastened the ties at her waist, allowing her petticoats and skirts to fall to the floor.

He eased her onto the bed and lay down alongside her. Heat from his hands skimmed her thighs. She arched against him, seeking contact for the part of her body that craved the most attention. The feel of his hands on her flesh sent a shudder through her. But it was nothing compared to the lightning bolt of sensation that jolted her when his fingers brushed her swollen, aching sex. He parted the lips, one finger slipping inside.

He leaned closer, pressing his lips to hers. "Eliza, I want to be inside you..." As he spoke, his finger slipped farther inside. He withdrew it and stroked her again, this time slipping upward to some intensely sensitive spot. Her hips nearly came off the bed from the shockwave of pleasure that rocked her.

She shuddered as he stroked her, then slid his finger back down and inside her. Over and over he stroked and teased, his finger sliding in and out until her hips began to move with restless need.

The feel of his lips tugging at her nipple and the thrust of his finger below sent shockwaves through her like an earthquake. She cried out, writhing instinctively as he pleasured her, embarrassed to realize the cries and mews she heard in the back of her brain were coming from her.

When she came back to herself, she realized she was kissing him, clinging to him like a drowning woman clutching a lifeline.

"What was that?" she asked, breathless.

His deep chuckle sounded in her ear. "That was just the beginning." He kissed her again and before long she was moaning with restless need.

At last he pulled back far enough to unfasten his trousers and slide them off.

He dropped a kiss to her chin. "I can't promise it won't hurt."

"I don't care if it does, I just want to be close to you, to know everything there is about loving you."

She shifted to accommodate him, sliding her hands down his back, over his buttocks. He eased forward. Heat filled her as her body at first resisted and then gave way to the size of him. He stilled for a moment, allowing her time to adjust. Pleasure skittered up her spine and all over her body as he retreated then thrust forward again.

A whimper tore from her throat. Her hands moved restlessly over his back, sliding over his buttocks, urging him closer. He rocked against her, lifting her hips to meet his next thrust and the next. She cried out, muscles clenching around him, squeezing until white heat bathed her insides in warmth and he shuddered one last hard drive into her.

Chest heaving with exertion, Coyote rolled to one side, pulling her tight against him.

She smiled, as contented as a cat with a belly full of fresh cream. His bare skin sliding along hers only made her eager to experience it all over again.

He pressed a kiss to the nape of her neck. "You okay?"

"Mmmm..." she sighed. "Better than all right."

"It will get better, I promise."

She turned to look at him. "I can't wait to find out." She shifted so that her head lay against his shoulder, fascinated by the soft hairs covering his chest. "Since you're going to be my husband, would it be all right if I called you Sam?"

He chuckled, the sound rumbling beneath her ear. "You don't like my nickname?"

She shrugged. "Yes, but everybody calls you that

and I'd like to be different." She frowned and raised her head to look at him. "Why *does* everybody call you that?"

He shrugged. "It's just a nickname I earned in the war. We all had names for each other—Badger, Fox, Wolf. Mine was Coyote for the way I could sneak up on enemy lines without being seen."

She sighed, fingers splaying in the hair on his chest once more. "Will I ever know everything about you?"

"You will," he assured her. "We have the rest of our lives to get to know each other."

Chapter Sixteen

The sun had already reached its high point when at last they emerged. They had spent the morning dozing, waking to make love then dozing again.

By some miracle no one had knocked on the door or had an urgent need to see the doctor. Still, Coyote needed to make his rounds and those would begin with Mother and Amethyst.

"She knows you're all right and I promised her I'd try to talk you out of leaving," Coyote said over a hurried meal of bread, chunks of cheese and coffee. "But I don't think she knows for certain that you stayed."

Eliza laughed. "The way this town talks? I'm sure she knows exactly where I am."

They gathered up their things and headed out to the waiting buggy. While Coyote brought the horse around, she stood there, studying the town. Church bells chimed a few doors down. It was Sunday and the town was quiet today. The peaceful sight suited her for some reason. In the distance, the train whistle sounded, reminding her of her arrival just a week ago.

Funny how it all seemed a lot longer than a week. When she'd arrived, she couldn't have imagined feeling at home here. Yet now, the sight of the town so quiet and still felt like seeing an old friend.

The ride to the Wyler County Social Club was

short. Coyote lifted her hand to his lips before they got out of the carriage. "Ready?"

She nodded.

"Mornin' Doc, Miss Eliza," Ruby called from the front porch. "We were wondering when we'd see you today."

As Eliza climbed the steps a smile broke out on Ruby's face. "Why look at you Miss Eliza, grinnin' like you won the prize hog at the county fair." She opened the door and announced their arrival.

Eliza frowned and looked over at Coyote. He shrugged, seemingly as puzzled by the announcement as she was. Nonetheless they stepped inside.

Ruby paused at the bottom of the stairs, smiling broadly. "We was hopin' we'd get a chance to thank ya, Miss Eliza. For what you done last night."

"What I did?" She shook her head. "No, no, that was foolish on my part."

Aoife hurried in from the direction of the kitchen and gave a small cry when she saw them. She rushed over to gather Eliza in her arms.

"I'm so glad you didn't go," she said, tears streaming down her face. "I heard the train whistle and all I could think was that I'd lost ya again."

Eliza pulled back, finding the woman's tears contagious. Aoife stroked her cheek before releasing her and turning to Coyote.

By now the rest of the house had gathered, at least those who were able. At the top of the stairs stood Abraham, Emerald, Opal and Pearl. As Eliza met his gaze, Abraham put his hands together and began to applaud. The others joined in.

"What on earth is all the fuss about?" Eliza asked

when they'd finished.

"You took up for us girls," Emerald said, her face beaming with happiness. "Just like Miss Addie would. We're just so awful proud of ya, Miss Eliza."

Ruby pulled her into a hug. "We girls are gonna want all the details about what Doc's like in the sack," she whispered. "We've made bets."

When she pulled away Eliza was sure her cheeks were flaming hot. She glanced at Coyote to see if he'd overheard, but he seemed oblivious.

A tall man came to lean over the upstairs railing, a smile turning up the corners of his moustache. "There's a lady up here wants to see her daughter," Russ Holt said.

She climbed the stairs, remembering all too clearly how strange this house had seemed to her just a week ago. At the landing, Coyote stopped to check Abraham's arm and then she and Aoife headed into Adelaide's room.

They didn't need words this time. Instead she moved into her mother's embrace and stayed there while they both sobbed.

When at last she pulled away, Addie brushed the hair back from her face and smiled. "So you're staying, then?"

She nodded.

"For how long?"

She glanced up as Coyote stepped into the doorway. "For as long as she'll have me," he said. "I asked her to marry me."

Adelaide whooped with delight. Russ beamed a wide smile. "I'm glad one of the O'Hanlan women isn't afraid to get married."

"Oh, you hush," Adelaide scolded. "Twice was enough for me, Russ Holt."

"So marry me anyway, woman," Russ chuckled. "Maybe three is your lucky number,"

"You know better." Addie shook her head.

He shrugged. "I'll ask you again next year. And then the year after that."

Addie waved a hand at him and focused on her daughter.

Aoife rushed over to hug them both. "I had a feeling I should have sent for Father O'Rorke the other day." She pulled back to study Eliza's face. "In fact, I think I should send for him now."

Eliza laughed.

"Tell her what else you had a feeling had about, Eef," Russ said.

Aoife's cheeks turned bright pink. "Now, now. All I said was that Adelaide needed help with that ankle. And with a handsome, single doctor in town it couldn't hurt to bring the girl here." She turned to look at the two, blue eyes twinkling. "The rest was up to them."

Epilogue

Six weeks later

The train whistle sounded and smoke filled the waiting area as the cars chugged into the depot.

Eliza stood with Coyote waiting for the passengers to disembark. "Who did you say was arriving today, Auntie Eefee?" she asked.

The Irishwoman shook her head. "I didn't say, that's why it's called a surprise."

Eliza frowned, but one look at her new husband and she forgot everything but him. She was exhausted but too happy to care. Being a doctor's wife was not easy, her husband was called out at all hours. But it was the time he was home she cherished most, when they stayed awake until the wee hours talking, making love and planning for the future.

She'd already met and fallen in love with the horse he'd named after her, and he had taken her to see the land he owned just outside of town where they would build their home.

Aoife nudged her as a woman stepped off the train. Short and stout, her dark hair liberally streaked with gray and a pronounced overbite. She looked a little uncertain as she looked around, her mouth set in a grim line.

"Aunt Cornelia?"

At the sound of her name the woman looked around. Eliza rushed toward her and after an awkward moment, her aunt opened her arms for a quick but distant hug. "What a surprise!"

"I've never had such an unpleasant trip in my entire life," Aunt Cornelia complained. "The seats on that train are so hard, the way those tracks jostle you around. Young man, you." She snapped her fingers. "Come get my bags."

Coyote raised his brows and glanced at Aoife. "She sounds a lot like her sister." Nonetheless he moved forward to take the luggage.

"Not just those—over there as well," Cornelia ordered.

Eliza gazed, wide eyed at the pile of luggage. There was much more than was needed for a brief visit. "Auntie?"

Aunt Cornelia came to stand before Aoife. "You're looking well. Thank you for writing me. I assume my sister is still bed-ridden."

"Yes, more or less, but she's finally starting to heal," Aoife said. They headed toward the buggy, where Coyote was still loading bags.

Cornelia drew herself up straighter and clasped her hands at her waist. "Well, she won't like me being there to care for her, but maybe it's time we mended fences."

"I agree," Eliza spoke up. "You two have stayed apart too long. You're sisters after all. It's time you made up. Life is too short."

"I quite agree," Aoife said, taking Eliza's arm and giving it a squeeze. "And of course, you'll be needing help, too. Once the baby comes."

"Baby?" Eliza stopped in her tracks. "Auntie

Eefee, I'm not—"

Aoife paused in mid step to look at her. "Eliza Jane Sullivan, I know an expectant mother when I see one."

At the buggy, Coyote dropped the bag he'd just been about to load. "What was that now?"

Aunt Cornelia regarded him with her sharp gaze. "You're a doctor and you couldn't tell?" She turned to look at Aoife and rolled her eyes.

They climbed into the buggy, Aunt Cornelia taking the front seat so she could get a better view of the town. "What's the place called again?"

"The Wylder County Social Club," Coyote said.

Cornelia looked this way and that, taking in the sights that met them as the buggy jostled forward. "Is it far?"

"Not at all," Eliza said. "It's just over the tracks, last place you come to."

"Does Adelaide know I'm coming?"

Eliza and shook her head. "No, Auntie. We thought it should be a surprise." She glanced at Aoife and gave a little giggle.

There was a beat of silence as Cornelia studied the bustling town around them. "Tell me again what it is my sister does?"

Coyote glanced over his shoulder, his gaze meeting Eliza's.

She smiled and winked at her husband. "Actually, Aunt Cornelia, you might say she runs a home for wayward girls."

A word about the author…

For as long as she can remember, Nicole McCaffrey has heard voices in her head. Fortunately, they're just characters wanting to tell her their stories. She wrote her first short story at age five (with a little help) and has never looked back.

She has been married to Peter, her best friend, for 22 years and together they have raised two amazing sons. When she is not reading, writing, or buried nose deep in a research book, chances are she is baking, gardening (aka planting things for the neighborhood deer to gobble up), or just spending time with her favorite guys.

Please visit her blog
https://nicolemccaffrey.blogspot.com/
for news, reviews, excerpts of published works and sneak peeks at upcoming releases.

Find Nicole on Facebook:
https://www.facebook.com/nmccaffreyauthor
Follow Nicole on Twitter:
https://twitter.com/NicMcCaffrey

CPSIA information can be obtained
at www.ICGtesting.com
Printed in the USA
LVHW021406021220
673103LV00001B/169